Slate Creek

Love Garden

Bruce Wayne Niles

ISBN 978-1-0980-5414-4 (paperback)
ISBN 978-1-0980-5415-1 (digital)

Christian Faith Publishing, Inc.
832 Park Avenue
Meadville, PA 16335
www.christianfaithpublishing.com

Printed in the United States of America

Dedication

It is to the three women I
have loved in my life.
My mother who Love me when I wasn't
lovable and supported me in everything
that I have tried to accomplish.
My sister who was always there
for me even though sometimes
we were many miles apart.
My wife who has been the joy of my
life in good times and hard times.

Table of Contents

1

First and Second

Little did I know, or even imagine, that a little slate creek could play such a large part in one's life...but it did. In fact, I do not remember it ever not being a part of my life. I know some people think it is a crick, but in this part of the country, it is creek.

First thing I remember is getting spanked with a willow switch for doing what I was told not to do and that was: "DO NOT GO IN THE WATER." My dad (Wayne) was a believer in the Bible verse, "Spare the rod and spoil the child." I know now that he disciplined me because he loved me, and I was too young to know, think about, or understand the danger of going in the water of the slippery Slate Creek.

The creek we lived near had a spot on the bank with an old log and a path down to the log made by my parents. They liked setting on that log and enjoying the beauty of the outdoors, reading, talking, and just being together. They watched all the wild-life that would come out as they quietly sat there. There were deer, rabbits, squirrels, chipmunks, woodchucks, ducks, geese, and a lot of land birds they identified by using a field guide bird book.

The second thing I remember has taken place at the old log spot. It was when I was eight or nine years old. I was permitted to run around and play while my parents sat quietly, enjoying the tranquility of the spot and the outdoors.

MOTHER. Bruce, do not go over by the creek.

I knew I wasn't allowed to go into the water. I had been allowed to go over near the water if I stayed on the bank of the creek. Mother must have meant something else other than just not to go over by the creek bank.

I was trying to get a flying grasshopper and ran to the bank of the creek.

MOTHER. Bruce, do not go over near the creek. Did you hear me? I'm not telling you again.

Dad sat there quietly and did not say a thing.

Well, if she's not going to tell me again and there's no punishment for doing it, then I can do it. It was not very long after she told me the second time not to go near the creek that I went over by the creek bank again.

I found it. What a great find. This is what she was trying to keep me from finding. I thought, I know why she didn't want me going by the creek. It is close to Easter, and somebody has already hidden some eggs for us to find at an Easter egg hunt. These were bigger than any eggs I'd ever seen, and there was a number of them, six or eight or more, lying there on the ground.

I did not have time to count them. I was about to pick one up when I heard a horn honk behind me. There are no roads down by the creek. There can't be a car down here. Why do I hear a horn honking? If you ever hear a horn honking when you are looking at a bunch of eggs, turn and run away from them as fast as you can; you are about to die.

The Good Book says to honor your father and mother that your days may be long. Knowing this, the opposite would be true also if you dishonor or disobey, then your days would be shortened.

Could I be about to get hit by a car? Could I be about to die? Because I was disobeying my mother as I was? Yes, it was because of a mother. Not my mother—a mother goose.

No. Not the Mother Goose of the collection French fairy tales and English nursery rhymes that teach you things about life. I did learn about life. I did think I was about to die by what seemed to me, at that time, to be a monster mother goose. She had to be as big as a horn blowing fire truck, and her wings were flapping. She was honking and charging at me. I knew I was going to be killed. I was going to die. I could not get away from there fast enough.

My mother and dad, for some strange reason, thought it was humorous and laughed as I was going to die by a monster goose. I did not die as I am the one telling you now about the thing I remember.

2

Stick Over Water

Sitting on the old log and reading with my parents did not happen to me as often as I grew older. I read stories about a big ark that held two of every kind of animal, fish that swallow people, a man that slept in a den with man-eating lions, and water that would part so you could walk to the other side on dry ground. You know, it had to be dry slate, not dry ground.

Many times, I wished I could part the water in Slate Creek and go to the other side. Later on, it became more important for me to get to the other side of Slate Creek. But for now, I was content to run around after the wildlife. Best of all was throwing stones in the water. What boy does not like the splash of a stone hitting the water?

I wanted to become good at throwing or slinging stones because one of the other stories my mother read to me was about a little boy named David that killed that great big giant warrior with a stone in a sling. He must have been good at slinging stones. I didn't know what slinging stones was at that time in my life.

I practiced throwing stones. I wanted to be good at throwing stones in case I was ever attacked by a big bad giant. The very, very best was when my dad taught me to skip stones across the top of the water. I became very good at skipping stones.

In my early teens, I was permitted to go down to the creek by myself. By then, I could swim but not in the creek, at least, not by the old log.

The water there was only four to six inches deep most of the year, too deep for a small boy that could not swim. But at age thirteen, I was five foot six and a one quarter inches tall. That quarter inch is important to a young man.

I did learn why my dad was concerned about me and the Slate Creek. Slate is very slippery when it is wet. More than once in over three or four years, I would come home all wet from trying to get to the other side of the creek. I tried to part the water by holding a stick out over the water, but it did not work for me like it did for Charlton Heston in the movie Ten Commandments, an epic religious drama film.

When I was fifteen, I made up my mind that this was the year I was going to get to the other side over wet slate or by parting the water. Sometimes God gives us goals to overcome things we think, like, "I cannot get through this. It is too hard." My mother said that God gives us goals that are just out of our reach. He will give us the desire to work to meet those goals because we can do more than we think we can. If we will trust Him and do our best, in time, we will see that it is good for our growth, and we can be an overcomer of hard things.

That summer, the desire was given to me to cross the Slate Creek and get to the other side. It would be very, very important to get to the other side of Slate Creek.

3
When You Are Alone

It was the first part of May, and I was down at my spot on Slate Creek, skipping stones. I am pretty good at it, if I do say so myself. Thinking I was the only one there to count the skips, I began counting each stone's skips aloud to a total of six, nine, eleven, eight, ten, and fifteen. My all high was eighteen.

After skipping a good count of thirteen, I heard a shrill whistle from the opposite shore. I looked to see who it was. I am telling you, I can be wrong a lot of the time as I was about to learn.

BRUCE. Hi, guy. What do you want?
PAT. Can you teach me to bump stones on the water like that? And don't call me a guy. IR a girl.

BRUCE. Girls can't whistle like that, and you don't look like a girl. (I learned I was wrong on both counts. She could whistle and she is a girl with her long blond hair tucked under a ball cap.)

PAT. My name is Patricia, but you **will not** call me Patricia, or I'll thump you hard. But you may call me Pat. I sit behind you in English class. We just moved into the house over here four weeks ago.

BRUCE, thinking. Oooh, it cannot be English. That is my worst class. She is new to the school and one of the best students in English class.

The boys at school talk about her being so good looking, all the ones who do not have a girlfriend. Some of the boys with girlfriends think she is hot but would not say it out loud. She is cute, very cute. I cannot say hi to her in class, she is so attractive.

Today will go down as one of the best days of my life. A great looker talking to me. Why is she talking to me? Am I only dreaming? I can't teach her to bump stones on the water. It isn't bumping stones, it is skipping stones. But if I correct her, she may never talk to me again. I want to talk to her again and again and again.

Dad told me that honesty is the best policy. If someone does not want the truth or can't accept it, get away from them. They will not give you the truth, and you should not trust them. I hope Dad is right, and God will work it all for good. I always tell the truth, no matter what the cost might be.

Wake up. She asked you a question.

It is called skipping stones. I can try to teach you, but you need to come over here on this side where the bank is lower.

PAT. No.

BRUCE, thinking. I knew it. I knew it. She doesn't like being corrected. She will never talk to me again. Why oh why didn't I keep my mouth shut?

4
Being All Wet

BRUCE. Please forgive me for correcting you. I hoped you would like to know the truth. It's called skipping stones.

PAT. Thank you for telling me that it is skipping stones so I did not make a fool of myself telling people that I learned how to bump stones on the water. I said no because I am afraid of the water. My mother, knowing my fears, would not like it if I slipped and got all wet, dirty, or hurt.

BRUCE, thinking. She has boots on. The water is low right now. How can she be afraid of the water? All she would get is a little wet. Water is a little cold at this time of the year. Does she want to be on this side with me to learn how to skip stones?

We could try crossing some other time, but I want to do it now. (Then it hit me like a typhoon. My desire was greater now than it had ever been before—and greater than I ever thought could be—to reach my goal of getting to the other shore.)

The goal to get across to the opposite shore is not only to get over there but to get back without falling, getting wet, and most of all, not looking like a loser. I want Pat to like me, not laugh at me, telling all the kids at school how I looked like a fish out of water, flopping around in the water.

She is standing there just looking at me, expecting me to be big and strong and to pick her up and carry her over here or to part the water like the Red Sea. I have tried that, and it did not work for me. I am only fifteen years old. Moses was an old man and had worked for God for a long time. He also had God's help. I did set a goal for this year: to get to the other shore but not with the cutest girl in school watching. That makes the goal ten times to one thousand times harder. I can't do it, can I? Okay. Okay. I am going for a flopping fish or glory.

I will come to you and help you to cross over. (Thinking positive should help.)

PAT. No. No. Not here where the slate is break-ing up and is too slippery with pieces on top of pieces. We would end up in the water. Did you not listen to me? I am afraid of the water.

If you will meet me up the creek across from our yard and give me a hand to jump over one spot, we can do it without getting wet, okay?

BRUCE. Okay. She did say we. I may be going up the creek without a paddle. With a short walk up the creek, and meeting her, will I get to hold her hand a short time? This can be a great day in my life.

PAT, reaching the spot. I told you this would be a good place. Hold out your hand so I can grab it as I jump.

BRUCE. First, I need you to agree to teach me to whistle loud like you do. Okay?

PAT. Okay. Okay. Now give me your hand.

5
Settled

PAT. Thank you for helping me over. (Stepping close to him.) You don't look like a girl.

BRUCE. I'm not a girl. I'm a young man.

PAT. Well, pardon me. You inferred that I was a boy because I whistle. So there, for you were thinking only boys can whistle. You asked me to agree to teach you to whistle. Not being able to whistle, you must be a girl. All boys can whistle. What about young men? Can they whistle?

BRUCE: I cannot whistle as loud as you did. I think I said "Girls can't whistle like that," which means I was incorrect about girls whistling. I did not mean you are a boy; your appearance was more like a boy than a girl.

PAT. You think I looked more like a boy? So you know what all girls look like? What all girls can do? What all girls think? How all girls feel? What all girls want to be and do in life? I think you know very little about girls.

You think I should wear a dress or skirt and blouse all the time. Something with frills and lace to be a girl? Why can't I put my hair up under a hat so it doesn't blow in my face or get all tangled? Is there a law a girl can't wear a ball cap?

BRUCE, thinking. What did I get myself into. She has fire. You thought I could not whistle. You were wrong. Besides—

PAT. Oooh, so I am wrong about boys, and you are incorrect about girls being able to whistle. You are like all boys thinking they are right all the time and thinking girls are wrong. What makes you incorrect? Why can't girls be incorrect as well as boys? Do you know the meaning of wrong and incorrect? Don't you like me? Are you mean to all girls, or am I special to be mean to?

BRUCE. I...I...I am not trying to be mean. It seems it is hard not to make you mad or, as you put it, be mean. Did I do something to make you mad or dislike me? Usually it takes two or three weeks, sometimes only days, for me to upset someone. With you, I hit my fastest time. (Looking at his watch.) Thirty minutes. Great. You helped me to hit a new all-time record. Thank you.

PAT. Now you are making fun of me too. You boys, who think you are young men, are all the same.

BRUCE: Please stop. (Thinking.) I like her fire. I don't think she is mad at me but at someone else. Please stop. You had said, "like all you boys, boys thinking they are making fun of me too." I am not "boys," "they," or "making fun of you too." I am not part of a group of boys or whoever they are, I speak for me only and just me. What group of boys are you making me a part of?

PAT, stops and thinks. You and my brothers. By the way, you should have seen the look on your face when I said, "You don't look like a girl."

BRUCE: I don't know your brothers. I don't think I have ever met them, would not know them to see them, and don't know how many you have. Do they go to our school?

PAT. I have two. They are out of high school. They are big, very big. Strong, very strong. And mean, very mean. That is why I was out walking. They made me mad.

When I saw you skipping stones, I thought I can learn to do that. It is a boy thing, and I can be better than those two jerks fighting about what a wife can or should do.

They love me, I know. Both look out for me and after me. They would thump anyone that might hurt me. But they are dumb. Dumb as a box of rocks. (With a little smile on her face.) I am not referring to the rocks you like to throw. They are as dumb as a box of rocks when it comes to knowing about girls. (Smiles.) I know because IR one. You remember that.

Bruce, *thinking.* I don't think I will ever think she is not female but a spitfire—handful, mad as a wet hen, and holy terror. In short, I should not make her mad.

Dad says a man is only as good as his word. Don't say it if you can't do it. To the best of my ability, I will always do what I say I will. You have my word on that.

I will try to teach you to skip stones. You did as I asked by coming over to this side.

Pat. I will try to teach you to whistle.

It is settled then. We are going to help each other. (She holds out her hand and they shake hands.) Okay, let's go. You know the path. You can lead us through the minefield to the skipping spot.

Bruce: What? What did you say about a minefield?

6
Mysteries Unveiled

PAT. Multitask. Can't you do two things at a time? Walk and talk or walk and listen? Let's go. You lead down the trail to the skipping spot.

BRUCE, thinking. As I think back, I remember her talking most of the time. There were those quiet times we enjoyed just being together. About thirty percent of the time, I got to speak.

(They start to walk to the skipping spot.)

PAT. How long have you lived here? We moved in about five weeks ago.

Do you have brothers or sisters? You know I have two brothers.

What work does your dad do? My dad is in the military. He will retire in about a year. My brothers are helping my mother set up the house.

Does your mother work? Mine is a housewife and mother. Dad said, "Those are the most important jobs I could hope to do in life." I would like to be a great cook or chef.

What is your favorite color? Mine is blue, like the sky.

Why do we need to be down at the water's edge? You know we could fall in.

How did you learn skipping? Is it hard to do?

How old are you? I am fourteen. I will be fifteen in July.

Are there bears out here? Would they eat us?

BRUCE, quickly answering. Not me. I can run faster than you. To see animals, you need to be quieter.

PAT. You wouldn't run and let one eat me, would you? No, you wouldn't, would you? You are picking on me like my brothers.

When did you learn to skip stones? I think I will pick it up fast.

Are you good at learning things? I am good at learning things.

Do you like school? I like school.

Oh, look, an open spot (to be known from now on only as the spot) and a campfire; a log to sit on. Can we sit down to rest a bit? Will anyone care we are here?

Can we make the fire bigger? I am a little cold.

Do you have something to cook, like hotdogs? I can cook hotdogs on a stick over the fire.

Bruce. This is my family's spot. I built the fire. I will put some more fuel on the fire for you. We keep cutting the brush back, making the spot bigger.

Pat, sitting on the log. I did not mean any-thing when I asked before if you knew the meaning of wrong and incorrect. I know you are not great in English. Remember I sit behind you in class.

Are you good at math? I am not good in arithmetic. If your good in math, maybe I could help you in English if you would help me in math, okay?

BRUCE. We can talk about that later. First, I would like to know what you were talking about when you said I could lead you through the minefield.

7

Minefield

Bruce. Your dad is in the military, right?

Pat. Yes

Bruce. Did you live in a country that was at war and had minefields?

Pat. No.

Bruce: Was your dad in a country that had danger because of minefields?

Pat. No.

Bruce. Is he now?

Pat. No

Bruce. Is it your brothers you are worried about getting into a minefield?

Pat. No.

Bruce. I know, I know. Is it because you heard all the explosions when I was playing with the fireworks?

Pat. No.

BRUCE. Okay. Come on. I give up. Tell me what you were talking about.

PAT. No, I don't want to.

BRUCE. Why not?

PAT. I am enjoying this too much. It's why I was upset and why my brothers were arguing. It is kind of a family thing. I don't know what you will think of us if I tell you.

BRUCE, holding up one finger, then two, then three. First, do you know what I will think of your family if you don't tell me? A half-truth is often worst because people think the half you're not telling is real bad. If it was good, you would be glad to tell it. Second, I don't believe I can think bad of your family if you are a part of it. Third, I would rather not start our relationship keeping secrets.

PAT, thinking with a little smile, holding her hand up a little over her head with one finger up, then two. First, are we starting a relationship? Second, will you tell me, and you need to be honest and truthful with me, who do you think is right?

Okay. (Taking a deep breath.) My dad was in a country where there had been a war, and there were minefields all over the land. When a family is walking, the wife is to walk ten paces behind the man. The children walk with the wife.

The debate was that if they had to go through the minefield, who is to go first? Dad, wife, or the child? My brothers said they would ship me over to go first because I am dumb, ugly, and will never be a wife or have children, and it would get me out of their hair. Other mean things like if I did find someone, I would poison them with my cooking. Those things aren't true. I am a good cook.

Who do you think should go first, husband, wife, or the child? Be honest and tell the full truth.

Bruce. Let me think about it. I want to get it right.

(Two loud whistles were heard from the other side of the creek.)

PAT. I got to go. That is my mother calling me for supper. This does not let you off the hook.

BRUCE. That was your mother whistling?

PAT. She is the one who taught me to whistle. Tomorrow I will whistle for you after I do my chores.

BRUCE. You mean like calling for a dog?

8
Sun, Come Out Tomorrow

The next day in school, she did not talk to me, not even to say hi. She did a lot of talking to everyone around me but not me. Why couldn't she at least say hi?

Her friends were around her like body-guards. I couldn't break into the group to say hi, not to the most popular girl in the school. I would look like a dweeb...or worse yet, a dork. (Yes, I know what they mean.)

English class was next. Surely she would talk to me then; she was sitting right behind me. She could just say hi as she walked by. There she came and there she goes. No hi. No nothing.

I am a loser, a dweeb, a dork, a low class from the other side of the creek. Why? Why? Why couldn't things go my way sometimes?

I did everything Dad was teaching me out of what he calls the Good Book. I went to Sunday School and church. I prayed. I tried to trust God and did His will. I tried to keep all those ten rules that were supposed to help you have a better life. I think I did most of the ten, whatever they were.

I was good to her yesterday even when she accused me of being mean to her. She blamed me for the things her brothers did. She was the one not doing things right. It was all her fault. All her fault. She could say hello.

I thought I was getting sick. I should should call home and have Mother come and get me. I couldn't afford to miss class if I wanted to pass English. Too late. Miss Norton was about to shut the door. Class was to quiet down; class was starting.

What? What did I hear in the silence of the room? Not reindeer hooves on the house-top but, yes, two little whistles coming from behind me.

I told you at the start of this: "I can be wrong a lot of the time." I do not know about tomorrow, but the sun did come out today.

9

Down Back

My alarm was about to go off. Half an hour later, I was awake. Not even drowsy. I got dressed to go cut brush down at the spot. I walked downstairs into the kitchen.

MOTHER. What are you doing up so early and on a Saturday? Have some breakfast. I put your bowl and spoon by the sink. Again, for the 2,034[th] time, when you are done, put the cereal away and the bowl and spoon in the sink.

     Are you okay? Are you sick? You could be a little flush or overheated. Sure you are not coming down with something? You sound like you are breathing hard, kinda like you are panting. Don't just stand there looking down back through the window.

Air doesn't go through the window. You need to open it. If you are warm, you may open the window to get air.

BRUCE. I could be a little warm. Think I will open the window and get a little air. I need to eat fast but not too fast. I don't want Mom or Dad to think I am rushing to get down to the spot. They will want to know why.

(Hearing two whistles.)

MOTHER. Stop right there, young man. For the 1,986ᵗʰ time, put your bowl and spoon in the sink.

BRUCE. But, Mom, I got something to do down at the spot. Can I take some hotdogs and stuff for lunch? I might be working. Making the spot bigger.

WAYNE. Jobs, obligations, and chores can be fun sometimes. Be safe and don't get hurt.

MOTHER. Yes, take some food; put it in a cooler bag. Be safe cooking around the fire. You're not going to eat all that food at one time, are you? Go have fun and be safe.

(Stepping over to shut the window.)
Silly boy. Doesn't he know I can see and

hear most of the things that go on along the creek and at the spot? For a little bit, I did not think I could get him to open the window. He would never have heard the whistle with it shut.

I am so glad I got to meet Mrs. Hawthorn at the ladies' fellowship tea. Glad she told us of her husband teaching the family to use hand signals and whistling to communicate with each other. She and her daughter miss him so much. Using signals make him a part of their lives when he is away from them.

She talked so highly about her sons. Too bad April didn't meet the boys before she got married and moved out of state. She could still be living here in town. She would have been too old for them. Oh well, she has a good family and is happy. WAYNE. The daughter could be a handful. Sounds like the girl is well-grounded, looking for true friends. Not ones that want something. I think Bruce and her can be true friends.

10

Woof, Woof

Running to the creek, I had to go through the spot. I stopped by the log to drop the cooler. Pat was standing on this side by the shore. Stopping, I watched her as she was throwing pieces of slate. I quietly walked up behind her.

BRUCE. You know, you throw like a girl.

PAT. IR one and I told you to remember that. Did you forget so soon?

BRUCE. Looks like it is time for your first lesson. Pick up a stone, a smooth one, which won't be hard, even for a girl. In that, most slate stones are smooth. Oh yeah, make me wrong by trying to pick up a big one. Hand me that one. I will put it up on the bank, and we will start getting them out of the way so we don't slip or trip on them.

(After a time of her throwing and me skipping stones, it was time to stop. She was getting the hang of skipping, and I don't need her getting better at skipping than me.)

BRUCE. Would you like a drink?

PAT. Yes.

BRUCE. There is an old pop can by the log you can use. I will get down and lap water up out of the creek. Woof, woof.

Hey. Why did you hit me on the shoulder? I just asked if you would like a drink.

PAT. You know why. You're being like my brothers. I only said I would whistle so you would know I was ready to come over. My family uses codes all the time.

BRUCE. You like me because I am like your brothers?

Hey. You hit me again. Don't you know I am standing here? Come, I have water and a bag for you. By the way, how did you get over the creek? I thought you needed my help.

PAT. I don't need a boy's help, yours, or my brothers. Or as for you, a young man's help. It is always nice for a gentleman to aid a lady by giving her a hand to support her. I said aid, not help.

BRUCE. What is the difference between aid and help? Don't answer that. We don't need to do English now. I have something else for you to do. (Walking over to the log and pulled out the cooler.) Something to drink and other food for the chef. I will start the fire.

I would like to take you up on your offer to help me with English, and I will aid you with math. Okay?

PAT. Okay.

BRUCE. I will try to treat you as a lady as long as you R one, and as long as you don't poison me, chef.

PAT. I can and will come over there and hit you if you keep it up.

BRUCE. If you just whistle, I will come to you. (Pant, pant.)

11

Curiosity

Things did not change much in school. We did not talk. Pat would be surrounded with her girl friends. From time to time, one of the boys would try to get though the body-guards and talk to her alone. That did not work as I could see. When I say see, I mean it because when she was near me, my eyes were on her.

Pat spent most of her time with girls talking and laughing, being giddy. Who knows what could be that funny all the time.

I looked forward to English class. Not because I liked English but because I liked who was in the class. Yes, most days, I did hear two little whistles, some time, some place, passing in the halls, by our lockers, getting on or off the bus. It was not her all the time.

I can whistle, just not loud. No, I had not learned to whistle loud yet.

In our time at the spot after school, we did study English and math. She did teach me some signs. When looking at me, she would put two fingers to her temple, meaning I am thinking of you. She was giving me insight into her family and things that outsiders did not know. Little did we know that a lot of the signs she was taught is international sign language.

The whistling signs are private. It did not matter then, and it does not matter now as it built trust in our relationship. Signing was for only us in our talks. Well, most of the time, it was her talking and me listening. She said one of her girl friends asked her:

CHELSEA. Why do you whistle?
PAT. Whistling helps my pucker. A girl needs a good strong pucker to be able to kiss well, doesn't she? I will be sixteen in little over a year, so I am going to keep prac-ticing. I may get to kiss someone, and dads do not count.

Getting to the spot as soon after school as we could to help each other with our homework. We learned we worked good together. We enjoyed each other, and a strong trusting relationship developed. Neither of us had told any of our class-mates about the relationship. I could say no one knew, but I would be wrong again.

12
Fifth Places

It was the first Saturday after school was out. I was getting some food for me and my chef. Mother came into the kitchen.

MOTHER. Bruce, you may not take food with you today.

BRUCE. Why not? I don't want to come back to the house to eat. Do you want me to go hungry?

MOTHER. Your Dad and I will be here at eleven thirty. There will be five place settings. (She waits for a response.) You will fill two of the place settings, or you can go hungry. We are happy for you, and we want to meet your girl friend. Make your mother happy and bring Patricia up for lunch.

BRUCE. Please don't call her Patricia. Please. Please don't refer to her as my girlfriend. I don't think she thinks of herself as my girlfriend. We are just friends. How do you know her name? Why do you think Pat is my girlfriend?

MOTHER. Silly boy. Or would you prefer young man? Why are males the last to know when someone likes them? As Pat might put it, dumb as a box of stones about girls.

The name you introduce her will be the name we will call her. Her mother, Mrs. Hawthorn, thinks she has a boy-friend. She wants to know the kind of boy her daughter is spending all her time with. Patricia, I am sorry. I will try to remember to call her Pat. Mrs. Hawthorn relayed to me Pat had said he is not a boy but a very nice young man. His name is Bruce. She sees him down by the creek at a place called the spot. She talks about him helping her with math. Can you think of anyone that might fit that description other than you?

BRUCE. No. You know Mrs. Hawthorn? How long have you known her? Is she nice?

MOTHER. We will eat at noon.

BRUCE. But what if—

MOTHER. No buts, no what ifs. Just ask her. She will come if you ask her.

BRUCE. Why do you think that?

MOTHER. I don't think it, I know it. Mothers know these things. Why do you think I will be setting five places?

BRUCE. Please tell me you didn't. Yes, I know you did invite Mrs. Hawthorn. Does Dad know? Yes, of course Dad knows. The only one that did not know was me.

MOTHER. Yes, your dad knows.

Back in the day when your dad and I were courting, your dad diddle-daddled too...all the time. I can say that. You may not.

He was seventeen when we met. I did not meet his mother and dad till he was going on twenty. He said that if it had been up to him, I would never have met his family or him meeting my family for fear of the unknown. The only reason he went and met my dad was because I told him I would not marry him till he got my dad's permission.

If I wanted Pat's family and our family to get to know each other, I should do something about it. So I did.

Did you hear the whistles? Go.

13
Put Down

Lunch time was good. It opened doors of friendship and understanding of our families.

Mr. Hawthorne was still deployed overseas and was not yet home. There were usually two members of Pat's family we would get together with, sometimes three or four if her brothers were not at their girl friends'. Neither family had other relatives close by, so our families would do things together, go to dinner, go shopping, and get together on holidays. I could ask Pat to do things with my family, and she, vice versa, could ask me to do things with her family. We got so relaxed with each other, and both homes felt like our own.

Sundays were restricted. Dad's standard is God first, family second, self third. Our family goes to church together, sits together, has lunch together. Before we go back out into the world, Dad would pray, thanking God for the past week and asking for God's guidance for his family in the coming week.

For Pat's birthday, our families had a cookout at the spot. We all had a good time. Pat had a great time because she outdid her brothers time and time again skipping stones and beating my all-time high of twenty skips by two skips. When I told her she had beat my all-time high, she said, "You must be a good teacher."

All in all, it was her day. She was right. She could and did learn skipping stones and is better at skipping stones than her brothers or as she had put it when we met, "the two jerks." Pat was right. Her brothers can be jerks. I learned that firsthand later that summer. Being a jerk is a boy thing, and we are good at it.

That August, I turned sixteen. Pat's family had a party for me. Our families, a couple of her brother's girlfriends, and six friends of Pat's and mine were included. After eating,

a cake was brought to me, and the tradi-
tional blowing out of candles and making of
a wish was done.

Shortly I was to wish Pat had been an
only child. Her brothers started to chant,
"He is sixteen and never been kissed, kiss him.
Sixteen and never been kissed, kiss him." I
know they were picking on Pat as much as
me, but this was not the time nor place for
a first kiss.

Pat winked at Chelsea. (Chelsea is the girl
that asked Pat about her whistling in school.
She had said, "Whistling helps my pucker. A
girl needs a good strong pucker to be able to
kiss well, doesn't she?") Pat stood up, looked
right at her brothers, and said, "I have been
practicing my kissing pucker." Reaching
over, she put her two hands on my cheeks,
and she kissed me on my forehead. "There.
A first kiss he will never forget." Then she
turned to her brothers and said, "Will you
jerks ever grow up?"

She was right. I will never forget my six-
teenth birthday or my first kiss.

14
Little Buck

Back in school, we did not get together as much as we did in the summer. As providence would have it, we had two classes together. Yes, English and math. We studied together throughout the year and accomplished more together than we could have separately. If you think that we studied together only to keep our grades higher, you would be in the same boat I am in a lot of the time. That boat is named wrong. Welcome aboard.

Once in a while, there was an activity in the school where you might take a date. There was homecoming, the fall dance around Halloween, all the sports games, and the big one, junior and senior prom.

The classmates knew that I was around Pat a lot, marking my territory like the big

buck and little buck in what is called the rut-
ting season or just rut. Males tried to pro-
claim their dominance and their male rank-
ing. Numerous times, I had upperclassmen.
Usually they were jocks. They come and tell
me they were going to take Pat to one of the
activities. I would say she has a mind of her
own and she uses it. You need her consent
not mine. Good luck. I knew they did not
have as much of as chance of succeeding as
a snow ball's has of surviving in, you know
where....

I do believe in hell and don't want to go
there. I also knew she was not permitted to
date singly. Her mother wouldn't agree to
her going on a date if there were not four
people. I enjoyed seeing the big bucks go down
in defeat. They learned to stay away from
my doe. I had the mother's seal of approval.
After I got my driver's license, I was permitted to take Pat to plays, music concerts at
school, and youth activities at church.

15
Official First

Spring had sprung. The water in the creek was down after the spring rain. It has been a little over a year ago since Pat and I met. It was my time to ask for aid even though I didn't need it. I was going to ask for help for the same reason I gave it a year ago.

I would get to hold her hand. Physical contact between us is a no-no, holding hands, hand on shoulder or arm. How do I know if she would like me to hold her hand? She was not trying to get over a creek all the time. If I was wrong, it could hurt our friendship. I didn't want that. As you know, I could be wrong a lot of the time. Again males are the last to know much of the time.

Our physical contact was limited to her punching me, which started close to the day we met. Why is it that girls can go hand in hand with girls, boy can slap boys on the butt, girls can punch boys, boys are not to touch girls at all? That is a very hard thing for boys not to do. Maybe my sister was right when she said girls don't touch boys or let boys touch them because "**boys have cooties.**"

Pat has taught me to whistle. Apparently, learning to whistle was harder than skipping stones, or I was a better teacher.

Going down to the creek where we crossed over, I whistled two times and waited for her to come. As she was about to step over:

BRUCE. Stop. Hold out your hand so I can grab it.

PAT. Why do you want me to hold out my hand.? What are you doing? Did my brothers put you up to something? You're not going to pull me into the water, are you? I was afraid of water, but I have been back and forth over the water so many times; I am not afraid now.

BRUCE. Please, can you be quiet and do as I ask? This is to be the official first time of me crossing over the creek, reaching my goal of getting to the other side of Slate Creek.

PAT. What do you mean?

BRUCE. Before we meet, I had set myself a goal of getting across the creek without getting wet.

PAT. What? You think you are going to do it today? You're not over yet. You could still slip and fall or get pushed in the water.

BRUCE. Shh. Will you help me? (I reach out my hand, and taking her hand, I steps to the other side. Reaching behind me pull out a rose. She then jerked back her hand. We came close to falling in the creek.)

BRUCE. Thank you for the past year. Please don't tell your brothers about the rose or the goal of crossing and not getting wet.

16
Growing Up

As our junior year was coming to a close, some questions needed to be answered:

Number 1: Are we going to the prom? No. Our church has a lock up for junior and seniors. It is not a couple's thing, but you may invite one other person to come with you. It will last sixteen hours, from five p.m. to nine a.m. It is a mix of girls' sleepover and a boys' night camp out. There were six on the planning committee with the youth pastor. We need to know what games, activities, and where and when to play them.

My chef worked on the food, supper, popcorn for a movie, snacks, and breakfast. Who knew there were so many questions that needed to be answered?

Number 2: Money. If I did my chores at home and kept my grades up, I got an allowance of ten dollars a week. Not enough money when you have a girlfriend. The prom might make it be official that we are girl and boyfriend, going steady, pinned, off the market, taken, spoken for, tied down.

Sometimes growing up is a pain. Good parents let you grow through the pain. Dad could give me a bigger allowance. Instead I got informed. Dad does not lecture, he informs. "A man is to pay his own way. Children live off their parents. When God gives you something or you acquire it on your own, you are obligated to take care of it to the best of your ability. Bruce, putting it another way so you do not misunderstand me, you could not have a dog because you could not pay for its food and shots.

"You have acquired a sweet girlfriend. If you wish to take the car to go see her, you will pay for the gas. If you want to take her out for a burger or ice cream or buy something for her birthday, you will pay for it. Got it? Go get a job."

Dad's informing and lectures are a lot alike to me. I am in need of a job.

Number 3: When do I get to spend time with Pat?

17
Doing

Meeting Pat at the spot, the first thing she said was:

PAT. We need to talk.

BRUCE. Are you breaking up with me?

PAT. No. Sometimes you are too much like my brothers. (She signed to me "dumb as a box rocks.") Besides it took me too long to get you to ask me to be your girl. If you had asked sooner, Mother would have told me I was too young to be going with someone, so it was better that you waited. You would have gotten a yes from me the day you brought the hot-dogs down and called me your chef. We do need to talk.

BRUCE. You mean, I get to say—ouch. Why did you hit me? I was only going to ask a question. Besides you hit like a girl. Ouch. I know you R one.

PAT. You blew it. I was thinking of giving you your first real kiss. Not now. You are being a jerk like my brothers.

I will not be able to spend as much time with you this summer. My mother insists I go to church teen camp first week of June. My dad will be coming home in the last week of June. We are to go back to his hometown where he is to be honored by riding in the Fourth of July parade because of the medal he was awarded.

We will stay for a week with his parents. That will be over my birthday. End of July, we are to go to Grandma Kirberger's for a week. Middle of August, my brother Craig is getting married. We will be there five days over your birthday.

School will be starting. I will get to see you a lot then, and we have four classes together, I think. It's our senior year; we will need to keep our grades up. We can study together, right?

Bruce. Right. We will. I need good grades to keep my allowance. If I can't get a job, we will have very little money for us to do things. You know what you want to do after school. Be a chef. I would love your input on where to look and what type of a job you think I would be good at doing. I don't know what type of work I'd like. What should I do?

Pat. We should pray, ask for a job. Trust God. Do your part by looking for a job.

18
Qualifications

That is the first time the spoken word love was used in our relationship. I knew at that moment that I loved her, not just liked her. That little seed of love with a hard outer shell of "You **will not** call me Patricia, or I will thump you hard" was planted in the soil of acceptance by "You may call me Pat." Watered by our friendship, our relationship has grown into a small plant of love. Dad would say the seed of love came from God, who is love. We are to love God first. Because he first loved us, his children. We are God's family. We are to love each other. We are brothers and sisters in Christ through the seeds of love.

I was down at the spot, clearing brush. I turned around to take some brush to the fire. I heard three whistles (meaning, "come here"). I thought, Pat was here at my house. She was supposed to be at camp.

I looked up and saw my dad signaling. So many times, I informed him code whistling is better than yelling. Whistles can be heard much farther and clearer. I went to see what my dad wanted.

DAD. Son, the spot is looking good. You have done a lot in a week. You need to stop working down at the spot.
BRUCE. Why?
DAD. You prayed and asked for something, did you not? You thought he did not hear you or he did not care. Today your prayer is answered...if you want it to be.

I worked on a man's car. Coming to pick his car up today, he asked me some-thing and told me something I did not expect. He stated, "I am the new man-ager at the old Westwood motel at the edge of town. So I don't waste my time, I rely on the knowledge of other people to help me. I am looking for a person that meet some qualifications to fill a job open-ing I have at Westwood. You have a good reputation in town as being truthful and trustworthy. Do you know a young man that will work hard, is honest, polite to people, can be trusted, will follow direc-tions as given, likes to learn new things, and could start working next week? He would be working with our maintenance man as a gofer.

"If you send someone, tell them to ask for Mr. Kiser. They will have the job if they tell me you sent them. Next week, we will run an ad for the job in the news-paper. They need to see me before then."

I told Mr. Kiser I know a young man working, cutting and clearing brush down by Slate Creek and is not getting paid. He will meet the other qualifications. He could start tomorrow. His name is Bruce; he is my son. Mr. Kiser stated, "Like father like son. Lucky for him I got my car fixed here. He has the job. Have him stop in as soon as he can for some paperwork. He will get paid very well for a teenager. If all goes as planned, there is a possibility for him to work part-time through the school year if he would like."

I said to Mr. Kiser that it is not luck but providence. Mr. Kiser replied, "You might be right."

19
Not a Moped

DAD. Bruce, do you think you fulfill those qualifications?

BRUCE. Yes.

DAD. Do you want to work where you get paid? That's called a job. A job is work you do for someone and they pay you.

BRUCE. Yes, I know Dad, and I'm not a little boy. Yes, I want work, and I would like to get paid. I know it's called a job.

DAD. Would you like to go for a ride with me and meet Mr. Kiser or take the car and go by yourself?

BRUCE. I would love for you to go along. I get to drive. (Dad's not lecturing or inform‐ing. He is just telling what he is thinking. Dads know just about everything.)

DAD. Have you read the 23rd Psalm? I know you have heard it. We have read it to you. I was thinking you must have made the Lord your Shepherd, and you are trusting Him. The neat part is all the other things that will take place in your life when you trust. You could not have asked for that job. It would not be made known till this week. You could not have known about the qualifications. Two weeks ago, you would not have met them. God needed to get you qualified. Did you pray asking for a job?

BRUCE. Well, kinda. Pat and I did. You told me to "go get a job." I put in some applications. I have no idea what I want to do or what I would be good at. Pat and I talked. She helped me see that I know two jobs I don't want to work at: the car wash or working at the Burger Barn.

We decided to just pray and ask for a job, trusting He would provide one that would fit me.

DAD. Psalm 23 says He will lead and guide us. You don't know it, but seeing you work, cutting and clearing brush down at Slate Creek, I could tell you are a hard worker. When Mr. Kiser said "will work hard," I thought of you. I knew you could meet all of his qualifications. When you two prayed and agreed to trust God and do your part, you did not know your part would be cutting brush, did you?

BRUCE. No. I was working at the spot because I missed Pat, and that is our special place.

DAD. I hope you learned a little about how God works. First he does hear us. There is an assurance at the end of that verse, saying surely goodness and love will follow all the days of your life. I think you have found the love of your life, and she may have also.

Fathers want what is best for their children, and we want you to meet your needs and goals in life.

BRUCE. But, Dad, she wants to go away and become a great chef in some big city.

DAD. As I started to say, all fathers, yours, hers, and our heavenly Father want the best for their sons and daughters, or if you prefer, their young men and their young women. I want God's best for you, my little skipper. (He called me a young man. I am a son and a young man and his little skipper. Dad called me a young man.)

Bruce. You have not called me skipper in a long time. Think you can still beat me at skipping? Better yet, do you think you can beat Pat? I don't think you can. She is up to twenty-four skips.

Dad. Is there something you would like me to help with?

Bruce. Like what?

Dad. Weeelll, like getting a skateboard, a bike, a moped, a scooter, a motorcycle, or a small car, or a small truck? Are you planning on walking to work? It's your responsibility to be on time at work, not mine.

We can talk about that on the way home. Let's go meet Mr. Kiser.

*****

Dad. Mr. Kiser this young man is my son, Bruce.

20
Consequences

As the summer and school year unfolded, everything Pat had said would take place did. That summer, Pat started looking for and applying at culinary schools.

Even after her dad came home, our families did a lot together. One of the best times we all had, I think, was Groundhog Day. Hawthorn's had a party. Each person put $10 in the pot. There were ten of use.

At the official start of the party, everyone was told the rules to the game. You need to do everything in twos, a takeoff from a movie Groundhog Day, where everything was repeated. You were to repeat and do everything in twos, you were to repeat or do everything in twos, everything in twos, everything in twos.

If you took two steps, you were to stop and then take two more steps. If you were to sit down, you were to stand back up and sit back down again. If you eat a potato chip, you were to eat two. If you had a sip of your drink, you were to take two sips. If you thought somebody violated rules, you could say stop, stop, and the group will decide if you've violated the rules. If you had broken the rules, you were out of the game. The person that went the longest without getting caught not repeating got all the money to use for Valentine's Day.

My dad, Wayne, won. You know he doesn't talk a lot anyhow, and my mother got $100 to spend for them on Valentine's Day.

I had started my job at the Westwood Motel in August. I worked with Perry, an older gentleman that worked most of his career in maintenance. We worked from the basement to things on the roof. I never knew what we were going to be doing.

When we had downtime, he taught me how to spot potential problems in the building and grounds. He was fun to work with.

He would tell me of funny things he had seen. Like the lady that had climbed out on the second-floor roof to help what she thought was a hurt pigeon only for it to fly away. She could not get back into her room through the window because she had slid it shut and it locked. She stood on the edge of the roof and threw pebbles from the gravel roof at people. She did not want to yell and draw attention to herself. People might think she was trying to kill herself. She only was on the second-floor roof.

Mr. Kiser asked me to stay on until Spring because we did the decorating for all the holidays, all but Groundhog Day.

Spring break was coming up in the middle of April. Pat and I were planning to spend time together and go on two-day trips. When my father informed me we were going to see my sister and be gone all spring break, I objected. Then I objected strongly by stating I will not go.

DAD. My house, my rules, son. You have always honored your mother and me. There are consequences to our decisions and actions. One consequence for not going will be not living in this house while we are gone. You will move out of this house before we leave. Trust me and honor my demand. Prove to yourself you are the young man I know you are.

BRUCE. What choice do I have? Okay, I will go on the outside, but on the inside, I am staying here.

DAD. Okay, son, but that attitude will change very soon.

BRUCE. How do you know that?

DAD. Because I spoke with Pat's dad, and I know if you were to ask Pat's parents if she could go with us, they would say yes.

I also spoke with Mr. Kiser, I informed him that I insisted you go with us to see your sister. You would be gone about three weeks. He said he was sorry to see you go, but he understood what was taking place, and he believed he could keep your job open for three weeks. You are to go see Mr. Kiser when we return home.

BRUCE. Dad, you're right. My attitude has changed. I'll be happy to go see my sister.

It was great. For two weeks Pat and I were together most of the time. We did things by ourselves, road the tram to the top of Sabino canyon and walked four miles back down, went to the zoo, Old Tucson, Desert Museum, Kitt Peak Observatory, museum of the old missile launch site, an open-pit copper mine site with huge big trucks, walks, and shopping. Sundays, we spent with the family.

21

Good for Goose

As soon as we returned home, I called to see what days I was scheduled to work. I was not on the schedule for the rest of April. May's calendar was not up yet.

I picked up my pay for the last days I had worked then asked to talk to Mr. Kiser. He was on vacation. Melinda, the office lady, told me Perry had asked her not to schedule me until I asked. Mr. Kiser agreed with Perry. Melinda said that it could be with me being a senior. I could use the time off. She heard that there could be some changes in the maintenance department. She did not know what they would be.

In May, for the anniversary of when we met, I got Pat two roses. We had planned to meet at her home to study for a final. Upon opening the door:

PAT. Give them to me.

BRUCE. Give you what?

PAT. You know what and if you don't give them to me right now, I will hurt you and take them from behind you. What color are they?

BRUCE. One is white and one is red. Please, please, please don't hurt me.

PAT. Here. Open this while I put them in some water.

I opened the small box. Inside were two skipping stones glued together and on the bottom was a heart and Pat. To this day, it is on my desk. But as we were studying, I noticed Pat was not studying. She was not talking; she was quiet. Something was wrong.

BRUCE. I can't keep my thoughts on our study-ing tonight. When I picked up my pay-check, Melinda said there were, or could be, changes in the maintenance department. I could be looking for a job after graduation. What is on your mind? (It was the first time Pat opened up and told me some of her fears, worries, and hopes for the next couple months.)

PAT. I did not dream of all the hoops you need to jump through, the time, paperwork, frustration, trouble, aggravation to find a culinary school and to be able to apply and get accepted to enroll in the school. I don't know what to do. I have applied at seven. One in Paris that we cannot afford. Four are full but would like me to apply again next year. The last has not responded at all. My hopes, my career, my life is falling apart. What can I do?

BRUCE. Are you asking for my input and help?

PAT. Y...Y...Yes.

BRUCE. I will not give you my input or help or advice but that of a very wise and insightful and very cute person. Ouch. Why did—

PAT. You know why. You are talking about me. So what would this insightful and wise person say?

BRUCE. She would say we should pray, asking for guidance in the fulfillment of your career. Trust God. Do your part by waiting, watching, and working as he works it out.

PAT. You pray first. I did last time.

22
Didn't Want

The week after graduation, I went to talk to Mr. Kiser to see if I still had a job. Mr. Kiser asked me to have a seat.

MR. KISER. As you may know, your father and I have become good friends and have lunch together every week. We both have management problems from time to time, so we confide in each other. Here are some changes coming in our maintenance department. The main one is replacing Perry's full-time position. We have someone in mind, but due to some state regulations, it will be this fall before we will fill Perry's position.

We are short people and have three positions open today, I am asking you to stay with us part-time. If you will, I will see you get twenty to thirty hours a week. If you know of a person looking for work, please let them know. We are looking to fill three positions and have them put in applications.

Can I have Melinda put you back on the work calendar, hopefully starting tomorrow?

BRUCE. Yes. I like the job and tried to do my best for you. Thank you.

*****

I got back home a little after noon. Pat whistled to let me know she was at the spot. I went down and I could see she was distraught and close to tears.

PAT. I heard from the next to last of the culinary schools I had applied to. They informed me I had applied too late to get in this year. My dad informed me that I need to get a job or do volunteer work.

I was not to stay at home doing nothing but waiting.

BRUCE. When I talked with Mr. Kiser, he mentioned he had some job openings. You could apply at Westwood.

PAT. I don't want to be a maid. I want to cook. I want to be a chef. I want to make people happy with the foods I make. I want family and friends to enjoy eating the good food I make.

BRUCE. You cannot make people happy or make them enjoy anything. You can make good food for them to enjoy. You might enjoy doing something besides being a chef.

PAT. Why can't you and my dad support me? Why are you trying to make me be a maid? Please support me in trying to become a chef.

BRUCE. No, I will not. I will pray and ask for guidance in the fulfillment of your career as we did before. Do you still trust God? Your father wants the best for you. He wants you to be happy, so do I. I never wanted you to go away. In fact, I hated the thought of you going to Paris. If you get accepted to the last school, I will be happy for you, not for me. That school is only about one hundred ten miles away. I could come to see you there. You could stay here and be a cook at the Burger Barn where "best beef on the farm is cooked right day and night."

Pat. I don't want to be a maid or cook at Burger Barn. I will try looking at other careers. We will trust God.

Bruce. Yes we will. Ouch. What did you hit me for that time?

Pat. I wanted to and you needed it.

Bruce. Dad would say, "You can't look up as you are falling down. You need to hit the bottom of the barrel first."

Come up to the house. You can cook us some lunch. Ouch. Why did you hit me this time?

Pat. I wanted too.

23
Tapestry

I came home from work and was going into the house. Dad was sitting down at the spot. When he saw me, he whistled for me to come to him.

DAD. Skipper, I would like to talk to you. (Well, I know I am not in trouble; he called me skipper.) "Mr. Kiser, Mr. Hawthorn, and myself were having lunch when the pastor came by. I asked him to join us if he did not mind being seen with Mr. Kiser, a very good friend. You know he does not attend our church. He is a member at that little brick church on the other side of town. We are trying to solve most of the problems of the world. We are starting right here in town. Your input could be helpful.

You are very good at solving puzzles, working out answers to problems. Let me tell you some of the things that were said. See if you can tell me what the pastor was talking about. I will tell you first what they see as a problem. Then I will tell you what the pastor said.

One man's wife misses not getting to spend time with her grandchildren.

One man wants to work only part-time.

One man wants to travel with his wife for a time.

One man's wife is concerned that her children would learn that a calling is better than a career.

One man wants to start a catering service.

One man wants to get out of the cold in the winter.

One man would like his daughter to enjoy the best career God has to offer her.

One man would like the person replacing him in his position to enjoy that career and be better at it than he was.

One man would like to help his son-in-law start a business.

One man's wife would like grandchildren.

One man would like to sell his house on a land contract.

One man's wife would like her son to stop being like his father and take some initiative.

One man would like to contract a salaried position with someone under the legal age.

The pastor said, "I pray you men can see God's handiwork all over this tapestry and the threads that will pull it all together. When you do, I would like to tie the knot."

BRUCE. Dad, I need to go. We can talk more when I get back.

DAD. Jacob, you will call him Mr. Hawthorn, will be reading in the yard down near the creek

BRUCE. How do...

DAD. You know the apple falling and tree thing? Like father like son thing.

24
Growing Plant

I was the first to know the things that took place the last two days. But then again, I seem to be good at getting things wrong. I would know after talking with Pat.

We were cooking out at the spot. Well, she was cooking or bringing the food. I was only permitted to eat the food and put wood on the fire.

BRUCE. The food looks good. I have the answer.
PAT. To what?
BRUCE. To the minefield question. Who do I think should go first, husband, wife, or child?
PAT. I don't want to talk about that. Can't you tell I am upset?
BRUCE. I think your brothers had it all wrong.

PAT. Don't you care why I am upset?

BRUCE. I think I know, and I am trying to do something about it.

PAT. Are you going to start a culinary school?

BRUCE. No, I am not starting a school. There are other options as in the minefield.

PAT. I got rejected by the last culinary school. Do you have any idea how that makes me feel?

BRUCE. Yes, and if things keep going this way, even more so.

PAT. What are you talking about?

BRUCE. The minefield, other options.

PAT. Why can't you understand? I feel useless, unwanted, a failure. My career is gone, lost.

BRUCE. Why don't you go for the better career your dad talks about?

PAT. If you don't stopping talking about the minefield or whatever you are going on about, I would pick you as the husband and send you first in the minefield.

BRUCE. That is what I am talking about— making me your husband and go around the minefields of life together. Will you marry me?

PAT. What am I, a consolation prize?

BRUCE. No. You are the prize, and I would be the winner. You would be a winner too if you love me like I love you.

PAT. Are you serious?

BRUCE. Surely you know I love you, Pat. In front of God and everybody. Since we are the only ones here, in front of God, will you marry me?

PAT. Before I answer you. I have already talked with my heavenly Father about marring you. He did not impress on me to say no; you had not asked me. I was afraid you were never going to ask me. Till I was asked, he didn't need to give me an answer of saying yes or no.

I want to know, did you talk to your heavenly father about asking me and did you get a yes?

My dad insisted that my brother go and ask his hopeful to be father-in-law for his daughter's hand in marriage. If you want my dad's blessings, and maybe my yes, you need go ask my dad if he would like you as a son-in-law first and then ask for his daughter's hand in marriage.

Bruce. I did and I did.

Pat. You did not.

Bruce. If we are going to start this marriage with you thinking I would lie to you, well... maybe I should withdraw my request for you to marry me. Ouch. Why did—

Pat. Shut up. If my dad said yes and you really want to marry me, kiss me.

Bruce. Well, he did not exactly say yes. I said to him, "I would like to ask your daughter to be my wife." His response was, "If she will have you, I and her mother would love to have you as a son-in-law." As far as me marrying you, I asked you first to marry me. If I am getting a yes and you want to marry me, you need to give me a yes and kiss me.

Pat. (Steps right up to me takes each of my hands in her hands.) yes. Surely you know I love you, Bruce. (places my arms around her and then kisses me.) How was that for your first real kiss?

BRUCE. Well the pucker was good, but you could use some practice on the kiss. Ouch. Why did—

PAT. Don't say it. You should know a love punch by now.

BRUCE. (Stepping closer to her, I took her hands in mine, put her arms around me and kissed her.) There, a second kiss we will never forget.

25

Give Up

PAT. Why did you never talk about getting married? When are we going to get married? What date are we going to pick? Do we pick a date now? How are we going to live? Are you making enough money for us to live on?

BRUCE. There are some things I need to tell you.

PAT. Where are we going to live? I guess I'll have to get a job. I wonder where I can get a job.

BRUCE. Our prayer was and is being answered. We asked for guidance, did we not?

PAT. I wonder what my parents think of me getting married. Did my mother know you were asking me? My mother would like me to have a big wedding, I think.

Do you want a big wedding? Dads pay for their daughters' weddings. He did not pay for my brothers, so they pay for their daughters', right? Won't my brothers be surprised? They don't know, do they?

BRUCE. No one knows you said yes but you and me and God.

PAT. Does your dad and mom know? Did you tell them? Who all did you tell that you were going to ask me?

BRUCE. Your father and my father are all part of our heavenly Father's plan.

PAT. What plan?

BRUCE. A plan I would like to tell you about. A plan that can answer most of your questions. A plan that could be implemented, or we could start implementing when you are willing to give up being a chef.

By your enthusiasm, I think you wanted to get married. Could be to anyone, though. Did not need to be me, right? (Goes to hit me but instead gives me a little kiss.)

PAT. No, you are the only one I have ever thought of marrying. What plan? What do you know that I don't?

BRUCE. I will tell you of the things I have learned over the last two to three days. None of this is written in stone or in slate as we might like to think. Then you tell me if what our God has done is not far and above what we ever thought possible. That he has been working for some time for you and me and will for some time to come.

26
Network

BRUCE. Our pastor ran into our fathers having lunch with Mr. Kiser. He was asked to join them. While they were having lunch and after listening to them, he said, "Don't you see God working in your lives, the lives of your son and daughter, and for each of you?"

My father asked me to sit down and talk with him. At lunch, they had talked about problems which stopped each of them from doing the things they would like to do.

I wanted to ask you to marry me but would not until I was able to provide for us. I did not know being able to earn a living and having a place to live was being taken care of by our heavenly Father.

Trusting and being patient is hard to do when you want something really bad.

I know my dad could see God laying out the answers to most of their problems. His talk pushed me to trust God and ask you to marry me before you got accepted by a culinary school. Fathers knew before I did that I would be asking you to marry me. Heavenly Father planned it, my father gave me the push, and your father waited by Slate Creek.

I went and talked with your father. He told me that he'd be happy to have me as a son-in-law. We talked for over an hour. He was confident I would be earning sufficient for me and a family soon. He and your mother wanted to do some traveling and were going to be gone for maybe six to nine months. They are going to see family and friends from the military services. They didn't know what they were going to do because at that time, you were planning on going away to school, and they had nobody to take care of the house. Your mother hoped that by the time your brother was a dad, they could spend time with him spoiling their grandchild.

If you did not go to culinary school, you could be home alone, and maybe could take care of the home by yourself? The house would be empty except for you, and that can be lonely. They were praying you might get married to a Christian young man they know you love.

I think he could also be tall, good looking, modest, with great sense of humor, patient, kind, hard-working, intelligent, good at skipping stones, can cross a creek without falling in and getting all wet, has a job, and loves you as much as you love him. That would be me. Right?

PAT. Yes, you are close enough. You will do. (Gives me a little kiss.)

BRUCE. Your dad would like to talk to you and your husband to be. Again, that would be me, right?

Talking about taking care of the house for a year or so when they would be traveling. Your dad suggested I talk to Perry.

He heard that he could be giving up his full-time job and wanted to train someone to take his place.

I talked to Perry. He does want to only work part-time for two to five more years. He could retire now that he is sixty-five, but he would enjoy training someone like me to do his job. He has discussed with Mr. Kiser the person he thinks would be great for the job. He suggested I go talk to Mr. Kiser

I went to Mr. Kiser and told him I knew Perry wanted to give up his full-time position. I asked him if I could have the job. He said no. I did not meet one of his requirements. He informed me it is not a job but a contracted position. You need to be of legal age of eighteen to enter a legal contract in this state. He informed me the position would not be open till the end of August. My name could be put on a very short list now that I have shown interest. He also asked me if I could help him. He informed me he was looking for someone to fill a position on his chef staff.

He wants to start a catering service and needs additional cooks. If I knew anybody to please have them contact him immediately.

Pat, do you know of any one that might be looking for a job on a chef's staff?

PAT. I did but they are working on setting up a wedding. They will need a caterer. I could go talk to him.

BRUCE. Mr. Kiser said I needed to talk with my father, which I did. My father knew they were looking at me to take over Perry's position because I had done a great job so far. He told me that the reason that we had gone out to my sister's was because my brother-in-law wanted to start up a mechanics business, and he wanted my dad to help. They decided he would need the most help in a year or two after he had built up a customer base and when all the snow birds were in town. My dad said these bones, these old bones, don't like the cold no more no more. They thought it would be good to go out there part of the year, help him start the business, and work with him. That way, my mother would be able to get to spend time with her grandchildren. But they cannot afford the cost of having two homes, one out there to live in part of the year, and one back here part of the year.

He was hoping that they could sell the house back here on a land contract to a new family that would let them keep one of the rooms to live in six months out of the year. Hopefully they will have some grandchildren back here they can spoil at the same time.

27
Box of Rocks

BRUCE. Like I have said before, our fathers want the best for their children. Sometimes it takes a while for children to know what they need, not just want. Do you know I did not have a dog or cat when I was growing up? I would have been responsible for taking care of it and pay for their food and shots. I chose not to do that; therefore, I chose not to have a pet.

My mother has a cat. She takes care of her cat. It is not my responsibility to take care of her cat. But it looks like we will become staff. Useful information, so you know, if you ever buy a house from your parents, and they get to stay in part of the house part of the year. We will own a cat part of the year. That is not quite true. Dogs look to you as a friend. A cat looks at you as staff.

I have chosen to have a wife, which means that I now take on responsibilities that I didn't even know existed. We started to work through all the questions that Pat asked when I first asked her to marry me. Over the next few weeks, we worked out most of the answers together. We had come to the understanding that we would be getting married the first of September.

Her mother and dad would be leaving around the tenth of September. They will be gone for at least six to nine months. They will travel to where her father had been in the service, meeting family and friends they have not seen for many years. We were to take care of their house while they were gone.

The following year, my father and mother were going to my sister's. We had made arrangements that we would buy their house on a land contract. The understanding was that their room would still be their room to use when they were in town. Yes, the cat would be my mother's for six months out of the year.

The wedding was a real interesting topic for discussion. It seems like everybody has an idea of how it should be done, where it's going to take place, and who all is going to be involved. It was all Pat's decision, and I supported her in every decision she made about the wedding, where it was going to be and how it was going to be done. I did mention that our pastor wanted to be the one, as he put, two tie the knot. Pat was pleased having him perform the ceremony.

Our heavenly Father knew Pat would want to get married at the spot. I did not know why I needed to spend all the time cutting and clearing brush down by Slate Creek. That summer, I had seeded grass and mowed the spot. We got a big tent and had a modest wedding. The pastor got to tie the knot, mentioned that day at lunch, that he would happy to tie. Not all the food, but most of the food, was catered by Westwood. Pat wanted a fire and hotdogs and all the fixings. There was no throwing of the garter.

There was no throwing of the flowers, but there was a lot of throwing. Pat wanted a box of rocks or throwing stones put on the pile of slate by the creek and challenged all comers. Some of the ladies tried skipping. I am not sure, but the wedding came close to being second place to her beating both her brothers in the skipping count.

The pastor tied the knot and everyone had fun.

28
Wrong Again

We went on our honeymoon. I won't tell you where it was. I will say a secluded lake, and there were lots of stones on the lakefront for skipping. The fishing was good, and Pat cooked some of the best fish I ever had. She said, "I do not fish." Not that she had anything against fishing for food. Her objection was baiting the hook and taking off the fish if she caught one.

Dad had taught me to do the unenjoyable then you do the enjoyable or work first then play. Later, Pat would not go in the water swimming. No, no, no. Not because she was afraid of the water. Remember she got over her fear of water. The water was cold, not just cold but icy cold. I was trying to be the big bad husband.

BRUCE. I am going swimming.

PAT. You are not and if you do, it will be over your cold body because that is what it will be. You know what I think about fishing? Your body will be there for a long time.

What is it people say, "God watches over babies and fools"? I am not a baby so that only leaves a fool. My wife must have been working for God that day. I am so glad she stopped me. That water was ice-cold. I am glad an angel, in the form of my wife, was watching over a fool that day.

Upon arriving home, we moved into the Hawthorn's residence where we took care of the property for about eleven months. When they returned home, it was not to stay but because Pat's younger brother was getting married. They came back for the wedding. They left the week after the wedding and went to her older brother's who became a father. They wanted to spend time with them and be able to spoil their first grandchild.

We stayed at the Hawthorn property for a little over two years, which was good because during that time, we did not have to pay rent. We did save money for the down payment for buying the house.

Late that September, my mother and dad did go to live with my sister and my brother-in-law for the winter so he could help with, hopefully, the extra work that my brother-in-law had due to the snowbirds coming in over the winter.

October first, we got to move into our home. That next week, my wife got sick, was throwing up, and could not go to work. Pat had not missed a day's work in two years from the day she started working. The days were cold when we moved in the house. Pat might have caught a cold by us moving in on cold days.

Pat had never lived twenty-four seven with a cat. I thought she could be allergic to the cat. Could it be an allergic reaction to the cat? The cat had taken to Pat right away and would be on her lap or near her all the time. I think the cat missed my mother.

By the third day, I knew I had to call my mother to see about getting rid of the cat.

I called my mother and told her how sick Pat was. I thought we should get rid of the cat. I knew both women would not be happy. Mom asked what are Pat's symptoms? She was nauseated, vomiting, would not eat no matter what I try to cook. Would not even talk about food or what I could get for her to eat.

MOTHER. Bruce. I am telling you Pat and my cat are not responsible for her being sick, you are.

BRUCE. Mom, I did not make her help us move. I am not a bad cook, just not as good as Pat. When did the cat get to be hers and yours?

MOTHER. The cat decided when it took to Pat. You need to talk to Pat.

*****

I couldn't talk with Pat at that time. She was lying down, trying to get some rest.

BRUCE. I talked to my mother. She thinks I am responsible for you being sick. How ridiculous is that?

PAT. I talked with my mother, and your mother before you got home today. We agree you are responsible. The test I took proved it. You got us pregnant, and you are going to be a father. (I was shocked, elated, and was crying tears of joy.) You may get the son you hope for.

BRUCE. I thank God for what he is doing in our lives. Why am I the last to know you are pregnant?

PAT. We women were the first to know I was pregnant, but you were the first to know we were trying to get pregnant.

29
Got It Right

Mothers are great. Everybody should have one. I got two, my mother and my mother-in-law. I have a great mother, and I have a great mother-in law. Both mothers were very concerned about Pat having morning sickness so bad that she could not work. Pat talked with her mother extensively about morning sickness. She had morning sickness when she was pregnant with her two sons but didn't seem to have any morning sickness at all when she was pregnant with Pat. She made a few suggestions on what Pat could do in order to minimize the morning sickness.

First thing that she suggested was before she got out of bed, she had to eat a couple saltine crackers. Stay hydrated by sipping diluted apple juice, slightly sweet lemon water with honey, slightly sweet mint tea. Snack often on bland food, such as rice cakes or just plain rice. Avoid any spicy food of any kind. She also suggested next time Pat plan on having a girl. Pat's mother had morning sick with her two sons and never had morning sickness carrying Pat. I got blamed for Pat being sick because I would like a son. All right, I might be a little bit responsible.

Let me say right up-front, my mother was not giving the best advice to Pat. Pat had talked with my mother. One of the suggestions was get bottles of ginger ale and drink small quantities of ginger ale all day or eat small bits of dried sugared ginger. She had used it and knew that old-time sailors would eat ginger to stop the nausea or sea sickness. It was good for motion sickness and stomach irritation. The not good advice given to Pat was: "Relax, take it easy, hold and pet the cat, have Bruce do all the cleaning, cooking, housekeeping, wait on you hand and foot for the next nine months." Thanks a lot, Mom.

My mother had morning sickness carrying me but none when carrying my sister. Drinking ginger ale and staying away from spicy foods was all she needed to do to keep from getting sick.

I had told my wife that morning sickness usually only lasted through the first trimester of a pregnancy. Two weeks before Christmas, her morning sickness symptoms started to let up. The week before Christmas, she had no morning sickness at all. From that point on and through the rest of her pregnancy, no morning sickness. I was right about the trimester. Of course I had looked up morning sickness and read about it, but at least I was right.

We started to work on the baby's room. I never knew there were so many different shades of blue, but my wife has a knack of putting different colors together and making them really look nice. As Pat put it: "I will be the designer, not the painter; and you will be a painter, not the designer. You paint at work so you can paint at home, and besides you are responsible that we are having a babies anyhow."

After the first of the year, Pat started back to work part-time. I had taken my lunch hour off and was going to go pick up roses. I always celebrated the day we met and still do. It was a good day that changed my life. Tomorrow is the anniversary of the day we met. Arriving back at work:

Perry. You need to immediately go to the hospital. Pat is in labor and is at the hospital.

Bruce. That can't be.

Perry. What do you mean "That can't be"? Surely you knew she was pregnant and has been that way for about nine months.

Bruce. I know she is pregnant. I was there when she got that way. She's not due for another two weeks. I'll see you sometime later. I am headed for the hospital.

Three thirty-three p.m. Pat became a mother. I became a father.

30

Shows

Mister and Mrs. Hawthorne and myself were in Pat's room when they brought her from the delivery room.

DOCTOR. A nurse will be bringing your daughter in shortly.

BRUCE, MR. HAWTHORN, MRS. HAWTHORN. What.?

DOCTOR. Why are you so surprised? Surely you knew you were having a daughter. You did have an ultrasound, didn't you?

PAT. We didn't ask the sex of the baby because we were sure I was having a boy. Our mothers both had boys and had morning sickness. But with the girls, they didn't have morning sickness.

DOCTOR. Well, if she was to be a boy, she should have stayed in the oven a little longer because she's missing a couple parts that would make her a little boy. She is a cute and healthy little girl. Here is the nurse now with your daughter.

PAT. What are we going to name her? All we have are boys' names picked out. Surely you know I love you, Bruce. I wanted to make you happy by having your son.

BRUCE. Surely you know I love you, Pat. I would be very happy with two Pats to love.

PAT. I would be happy with two Bruces. What do they call it when a little girl's name is the same as her mother's? It's not junior, is it? When father and son are named the same they are called junior, right? I don't think I want her to be named Pat after me.

BRUCE. Surely you don't want her to be named Bruce after me. Do you? We don't want her to grow up thinking we did not want her or we do not love her because she is a girl. I should say, before we knew we had a daughter.

PAT. What about the name Shirley? Surely she shows our love for each other, and we love her and want her to know she has always been loved by us.

BRUCE. Can we spell her name surely, as in "Surely I love you, Dad"? I would like that.

PAT. "Surely I love you, Mom." I like it too. What do you think, Mom and Dad?

The Hawthorns agreed that the name would be very fitting. "If Surely could ever realize the true love that brought her into being and how much she was loved by the two of you and by us and her other grandparents, it would be the greatest gift that you can give a child. Just to know that they are loved, have always been loved, and will always be loved."

31
Your Daughter

Pat took maternity leave so that she could care for Surely for the first year, part of it without pay. Pat started back to work part-time, and her mother babysat Surely when Pat was working. About two months later, my parents returned from my sister's and stayed at my home. So the two grandparents took turns taking care of Surely.

One day, when the grandmothers were having lunch together and taking care of Surely, my mother noticed that she was acting what she thought was strange. She said to Pat's mother, "What's wrong with Surely? Why is she doing that?" Pat's mother responded, "She is signing that she would like a drink. She has learned some sign language from us and also from the kids' TV shows she watches. They do some sign language, and she has learned that it's easier to use sign language than it is to pronounce some of the words.

I will say that was some of the quieter times of raising Surely. Surely was a lot like her mother in many ways. One, she likes asking questions, wants to know this, wanting to know that, did you see this and what's that and where are we going, and on and on.

A year later on, April 1, known as April Fool's Day, when I came home, my wife said, "You need to talk with your daughter." Now when she is referred to as "my daughter," there's something that's not going right.

Bruce. About what? (Thinking I am being set up for some kind of April Fool's prank, how can I be wrong about that? It's April first, and Pat has a good sense of humor)

Pat. Your daughter came out of the laundry room earlier today, shaking both of her hands, saying, "No like, no like, no like." She had been playing in the cat's litter box and got into where the litter was wet and had it all over her. Her hands were full of wet litter. She was shaking her hands, throwing wet litter all over the little laundry room. Don't you dare laugh; it's not funny.

Bruce. So what do you want me to do? Get rid of the cat? Get rid of just the litter box, which isn't going to help. The cat that needs to go somewhere. You don't want me to get rid of my daughter, do you? What do you want me to do? What am I going to talk to her about? She is only two and half.

Pat. Talk to her and you will find out why she did it. And you can fix it. Then I will have my good little daughter back. (Giving me a kiss on the cheek.) Talk to her.

Surely, seeing him getting a little kiss. Me too. Me too. Me too.

Bruce. Surely, you know I love you. Did you do something bad today?

Surely. No like.

Bruce. Did you make Mommy not happy today? Okay. Pat, you need to interpret or translate what she's trying to tell me. I cannot understand this signing she's trying to do.

Pat. On one of the kids shows today, they were telling kids about planting a garden and digging in the soil. I think what she is saying is that she wants to dig. I think the other symbol she's using is to plant or place in the ground. I think she just wanted to play in the soil, and the only dirt that was available for her was in the cat litter box.

Bruce. Surely, do you want to dig in the dirt and plant something? Is that what you saw on TV? Do you want to do as they did on TV?

Surely, shakes her head. Yes.

It was agreed that day that she would no longer play in the cat's box, and we would dig up a place in the spot where she could play, dig, and we planted a garden.

32
Pets

We did not know a lot about planting a garden. Most of what we knew, I would call a biblical reference, which was: "As a man plants or sows that shall he also reap." (Genesis 1:11–12, NAS) Then God said, "Let the earth sprout vegetation, plants yielding seed, and fruit trees on the earth bearing fruit after their kind with seed in them;" and it was so. 12 The earth brought forth vegetation, plants yielding seed after their kind, and trees bearing fruit with seed in them, after their kind; and God saw that it was good.

We see the importance God puts on planting and harvesting in Galatians 6:7, "Be not deceived God is not mocked for whatsoever a man soweth that shall he also reap." We tilled a small plot and planted a few seeds.

Surely enjoyed her plot that summer more than we did and got more out of her garden. Her's were not good to eat. She had mud pies, mud cakes, mud cookies all dried in the sun and one fairly muddy child for a good part of the summer. She did enjoy playing and digging.

We had learned from the first year that the area down by the spot was an excellent place for a garden. We did very well on the small spot, so we enlarged it quite a little bit. We had good crops that year of many different things: peas, carrots, beans, squash, corn, and tomatoes.

The most memorable thing about that year's gardening was this:

One day, after working in the garden, we returned back to the house. Pat took Surely into the bathroom to give her a bath and clean her up from all the earth that covered her foot to head.

I heard an extremely loud and shrill scream and then a loud long whistle, which basically means, "I need help." Running into the bathroom, my wife was standing up on the commode.

PAT. Take care of your daughter.

On the floor were fifteen to twenty large earthworms, a couple small snails, and one small toad. They were crawling around on the floor by the tub. Surely had picked them up in the garden and put them in her pocket. When my wife took her daughter's clothes off, they fell out of her pocket onto the floor.

SURELY. Me pets. I like wiggly.
BRUCE. Surely you know I love you, Surely. Mommy has something she would like you to do and some bad news about your wiggles. Don't you, Pat?
PAT. I love you, Surely. Mommy does not like wiggly pets. Will you pick up all your pets, and Daddy will take you and them down to the garden where your pets will be happy to live.
SURELY. Can me keep Hoppy?

PAT. No. The toad will be happier in the garden.

We learned that Pat still did not like worms. But that my daughter enjoyed worms and probably would enjoy fishing.

33
Cover-Up

One of Surely's third grade projects, or requirements, was to do a show and tell. This was in early spring, so she chose the topic of gardening. I wouldn't say that she was excited about it, but she talked so much about gardening, what she had done, what we had planted in the garden, and how the vegetables are good food.

The teacher had asked her three times to please finish and take her seat. She still hadn't finished with all the details of what she had done in our garden and all her wiggly pets when the last bell of the day sounded. She had to stop talking, or they might still be listing to her talking about our garden.

I rototilled the garden, getting it ready for planting. I went back up to the house.

Surely. Dad, are we getting ready to plant the garden again?

Bruce. Yes.

Surely. Can I help laying it out and planting it this year?

Bruce. Yes, you may.

Surely. Why don't we plant the garden up by the house? Why do we have it down back?

Bruce. The soil down there is usually a little more moist, and we're right near the creek, where we can get water if the summer is too dry, and we need to water the plants.

The spot is a special place. My mother and dad used to sit there and relax, read, and enjoy God's creation. They still do from time to time. The spot means a lot to our families. The place where the garden is, your mother and I cleaned all the brush off, and that's where we had the tent.

Surely. What tent?

Bruce. Your mother and I got married at the spot near a tent that we had our reception under.

Surely. Why did you get married down there?

Bruce. Your mother and I met down near the spot.

Surely. Does that mean I'll meet somebody down there and get married to him?

Bruce. No, I don't think so. Your mother lived on the other side of the creek, where your grandma and grandpa live.

Surely. Do I get to pick what we will grow in the garden?

Bruce. Why do ask?

Surely. I don't want to grow any of those little baby cabbage things.

Bruce. You mean brussels sprouts?

Surely. Yes. How do you know what it's going to grow to be when you plant something?

Bruce. What the seed is that you plant is what will grow. If you plant a kernel of corn, you will get corn. If you plant a pea, you're going to get peas. Whatever you plant is what you're going to get. God worked it out that way. You plant something, you get many times more of it back than you planted.

Surely. How can God see what we plant when we cover it up?

Bruce. If I put a blanket over your head, like at night when you go to bed, do you still know you are Surely?

Surely. Yes.

Bruce. Surely you know I love you, Surely. Even when I don't say it, you know I love you, don't you? God puts things in us like he does with seeds that makes us what and who we are. When we plant a seed, we get to see what God put in it. But always, you get what you plant and more of it.

Surely. Yes, I know. Surely you know I love you, Dad, even when I don't say it. Does Mom know I love her even when I don't say it?

Bruce. Yes, she does. But she still likes you to tell her also.

Saturday we will go to the store and look for seeds. Most of the seeds will have a picture on them to help us know what we will be growing in the garden.

34
Family Affair

The next day, we went to the store, looking at all the seeds there were for gardening. Surely's eyes lit up. She got excited like it was a candy store or toy store or Christmas time. She couldn't believe all the different kinds of seeds and plants there are that she could plant in her garden. (By now, it was her garden.)

This young lady had a passion for gardening like her mother had for cooking when her mother was young. Just so I don't get in trouble, let me restate that, when her mother was younger. She stills has that passion today.

We spent a lot of time as a family in the garden in those years. Growing plants really got into Surely's blood. She was really excited about gardening. I told her she can pick eight to fifteen different seed packs that we would plant, and we would come back and get a couple different plants when the plants were for sale. She was content with that but not particularly happy.

This became an annual family affair, planting the garden. I meant, not only her mother and me, also the grandparents. We learned really quickly that it was Surely's garden. We would sit at the spot some-times, build a fire, read, or just watch her, or wait until she asked for help before we got involved. We all enjoyed watching her and helping her take care of her garden.

One thing that Surely was not happy about was once you planted the seeds, you couldn't see them. She didn't know what was planted there. She took the seed enve-lopes that had the pictures and put them on little stakes by each section of planting so she could tell what was planted. She said, "I know God knows what is planted there but I don't. So I'm going to help him out so that he doesn't have to tell me. I'll be able to look at the picture."

The problem with that is by the middle of the summer, the packets had been rained on and started to deteriorate. The wind would blow them away. She wasn't happy with that, so she started making signs out of cardboard that she would put on the end of each section. That did not solve the problem either. This was a problem that she wanted to solve. She must have spent a lot of time thinking about it over the winter.

Springtime, she went down to the pile of slate that was by the side of the creek and brought a couple flat pieces up to the house. She started with putting the names on in chalk, which did not stay. It would wash right off. She tried magic markers, which stayed a little better. Still didn't solve the problem altogether.

Next, I noticed that she had a hammer and a screwdriver, and she was trying to carve the names of the different plants into the slate. This was working. She had made up her mind—she was going to have signs there that would stay so that she would know what was planted.

At work, we had a tool called a Dremel, which had a grinder bit that actually would cut into stone. Slate is very soft, and the little grinders would cut the slate fairly easy. I brought one home to try. She fell in love with it. It did just exactly what she wanted it to do.

35
Weeds

The next day, when I came home, Surely met me at the door.

SURELY. Where is that cutting thing? I want to put names on slate.

BRUCE. Surely, you know the Dremel was not mine. I borrowed it from work. Mr. Kiser allowed us to try it to see if it would work. I gave him my word that I would bring it back the next day. I had to take it back to work. That's who owns it, and that's where it needs to be.

SURELY. But, Dad, I want to use it now.

BRUCE. When you give somebody your word and you tell them you're going to do something, you need to do it, if at all possible. Let me put it this way. If you got a package of seeds and you planted them and they all came out weeds instead of the vegetables, would you be happy?

SURELY. No.

BRUCE. No, you wouldn't. Your words are like seeds you plant. You say you're going to do something and you don't do it, it's like your words are weeds. It's no good. It's useless and people won't trust you.

Your granddad taught me honesty is the best policy. You say it, you do it, and if someone does not hold to their word, they cannot be trusted. Get away from them. Do you understand?

SURELY. I think so. Don't use bad seeds, or you will get weeds. Use good seeds.

BRUCE. Surely, it's okay to want something. You cannot keep what belongs to somebody else. I know you would like a Dremel of your own. You need to figure out how to get one of your own. You could start by saving your allowance or figure out some other way to acquire one.

SURELY. Dad, if you loved me, you would get me one.

Bruce. Surely know I love you, Surely. Is that all I mean to you? Someone that gives you things what you want? Pray about it. You can and should make our requests or wants known to our heavenly Father and your earthly father.

We do love you, but that does not mean we will give everything you ask for when you ask for it. Some things may not be good for you. As fathers, we look out for your good, just not gust your wants.

Surely, wanting something is kind of like planting a seed. You plant a seed, but you don't have the vegetable right then. You will have to wait for it to grow. When you want something, you plan for it, you work for it, you do the best you can to acquire it. Then you let God work out the growing and developing. You have to do your part first. I do love you, but I'm not going to buy your love with things.

36
Corner

That weekend, my wife and I were on the back porch talking. Surely was down in the garden. You can hear voices from the porch down back at the spot. So we stopped speaking and started using signs to communicate back and forth. We would do this sometimes when we did not want people to know what we were talking about. But this time, I wanted Surely to be curious enough to watch and see what we were communicating about.

Knowing that you can see a lot farther than what you can hear, my wife and I continued to sign about things for Surely's birthday, but all were things that we knew she would not necessarily want, such as shoes, socks, other different clothes, dolls, and other toys. Sure enough, Surely was watching, and

I know she could tell at that distance what we were talking about—the things she could be getting for her birthday. We did not talk about anything that had to do with the garden or the signs or the Dremel.

We planned to have the grandparents for a birthday supper for Surely. After eating, each of us would present her with a birthday gift, things that she was not excited about getting. All the things we had signed about except for one—a doll.

The final adult to present her with a present was her Grandma Hawthorn. Giving her a card that read inside: "I put your present over in the corner by the stand." Surely went over to the corner to find a present, assuming that it was going to be a doll.

SURELY. Yaaay. I got it, I got it.
BRUCE. What are you screaming about? Did you see a mouse? Did you catch a mouse?
SURELY. You know I didn't get a mouse. You know I got the cutting thing I wanted. You're the one responsible for all this aren't you, Dad? You are mean to make

me think I wasn't getting the cutting thing.

BRUCE. Life doesn't go the way we would like it to all the time. No, we all wanted to see the surprise on your face and how happy we thought you would be. We all love you and want you to be happy.

SURELY, walks to each of them and gives each a hug and a kiss. Surely know I love you, Mom.

Surely know I love you, Dad.
Surely know I love you, Grandpa.
Surely know I love you, Grandma.
Surely know I love you, Grandpa (Hawthorn).
Surely know I love you, Grandma (Hawthorn).

No cake, no ice cream for Surely. She was too busy checking out the Dremel, finding out what the parts were and looking at the manual to see how it was put together and how it worked. She wanted to go get a piece of slate and start carving right now. She was told to wait until the party was over.

37
Unwelcomed Visitors

When the garden was ready to plant, she made slate markers for all the different vegetables in the garden and knew where they were going to be planted. That year, her signs lasted the whole year long. But even though her slate signs had lasted the whole year and would last for years to come, she wasn't happy with them. They were just simple signs with names on them.

That winter, she spent time putting fancy designs on the slate, along with putting the names in different types of lettering so that they were pretty, as well as informative. The old slates were put in a pile alongside the walkway going down to the spot.

The next year was the same as what had been for a number of years already. I got to rototill the garden and got it ready for planting. From that point on, Surely and Pat were the ones who were in charge of planning, designing, and laying it out. I don't know who enjoyed the garden more, my wife or my daughter. They got to spend time with each other, doing something they both loved. My wife got the benefit of having fresh vegetables and spices for her cooking, and my daughter got to do the planting and to make all the signs for the different plots.

We found out that Surely was a skilled artist and soon started to not only put names and fancy designs on the slate but also designs of the vegetables that were being planted. Surely had started to do designs on the slate of different animals, like rabbits and woodchucks and deer. All of them had circles on them that she painted red with a red line down across them.

Yes, she had some unwelcomed guests. Just so you know, rabbits, woodchucks, and deer don't read signs. You know it says no rabbits, no deer, no woodchucks, but they still come in and eat your garden.

Surely you know everything that God made has its purpose and its reason for being. We don't understand sometimes the circumstances or why things are the way they are. God has a greater plan and sooner or later, it all comes together like one great big puzzle. Then we can see parts of his plan. He made animals for us to eat, for us to enjoy watching, and for us to have as a pet.

Granddads come to the rescue by putting up around the garden some fencing with flags on the lines, trying to keep the deer out and give some other unwelcomed guests a different place to live a little ways from there. Granddads set live traps (traps that do not hurt but hold an animal), placing them in the garden, catching the rabbits and woodchucks. They got a total of seven rabbits and three woodchucks that year, and they were all moved about ten miles away into a wooded area.

38
Slate Dog

Her slate signs became a record of all the things that went on in the garden. Pictures of rabbits eating the plants, pictures of her granddad setting out the traps. Everyone that came to the house had to go through the garden. All of her classmates that would come over to study. Before you started to study, if you hadn't been down to the garden before, you were strongly encouraged to go down and see the garden even to the point, I would say, of being forced to before anything else could be done. You would also get a verbal rendition of everything that had taken place at the garden spot.

Her art teacher had come specifically to see the garden. She had heard about all the good artwork that Surely was doing on the slate. "Surely, you are a very skilled artist and could very possibly make money at selling your art slates."

If you came to the house and went to see the garden spot, you got your name put on a slate with all the other people that had visited the garden. Even if it was in the winter when there was no garden to see, you got a verbal update on what is coming in the spring.

Not just people. The pastor had brought his dog so he could run a little bit up and down the creek. The dog got her name and her likeness engraved on a piece of slate.

Over the school years, there were a couple girlfriends that would come and hang out quite a lot with Surely. There were also two boys named Tony and Leroy.

Tony's excuse for coming was that he wanted to learn how to do the slate sculptures. He wanted her to teach him, so he was there off and on all year long.

Leroy's excuse, on the other hand, was that he wanted to learn gardening and wanted to help her with a garden.

You and I both know that the primary reason the both of them were there was not to learn slate carving or to do gardening but interest in Surely.

It was not uncommon for her and her classmates to have parties or a get together or just hang out down at the spot near the garden. We were starting to run out of good stones for skipping at the spot and sometimes had to go up and down the stream to get stones to skip. Larger pieces of slate had to be put on the pile so she would have additional slate. She would only use the slate one time, and then it would go on the used slate pile.

Surely had decided that the following year, she not only would have fruits and vegetables, but she was also going to raise different kinds of flowers and have flowers around the garden. She had heard that certain animals did not like the smell of certain flowers; therefore, they would not come into the garden area. She thought it was worth a try to keep out some of the unwanted guests.

39
Waiting Room

JIM. Bruce, Mr. Kiser wants you to stop whatever you're doing and come down to his office immediately.

*****

BRUCE. Mr. Kiser, you wanted to see me?

MR. KISER. Yes, Bruce, come in and have a seat, please. Please shut the door behind you. I know you know Trooper Brown, correct? (Points to Trooper Brown in the room.)

BRUCE. Yes, my daughter and his son are good friends. His son is over to my house quite a lot.

TROOPER BROWN. Bruce, I have some bad news, your daughter and wife are alive, but they were just in a terrible car accident. Both have been moved to trauma centers. Your wife to the trauma center here in town, your daughter is being life flighted to Children's Hospital trauma center.

BRUCE. Pat was picking up Surely early from school. They were going to go to the hairdressers. Surely wanted to get her hair done for the junior senior dance tomorrow night. Your son is taking her, and Pat and I are to be chaperons. What happened? Who's at fault? Where did it take place? I need to go to the hospital to see my wife.

TROOPER BROWN. In just a few minutes, I can take you down to the hospital, but your wife is in the ER or in surgery. I would assume at the moment, you wouldn't be able to see her or be with her at this time anyhow.

As far as what took place, we don't know precisely, but the preliminary information that we have is that two boys were riding their bikes, jetted out into the road and into the path of a truck that was coming toward your wife. He swerved to keep from hitting the boys, sideswiping the one boy, throwing him and his bike onto the side of the road. But in so doing, he came in contact with the back of your wife's car, making the car swing around and was hit by the back of the truck, causing the car to roll over a number of times and land in the ditch. That's why your wife and your daughter are so badly injured, because of the flipping and rolling of the car.

The driver saved the lives of two boys, but in doing so, the cost was put on your wife and daughter.

There was a man at the scene that said he was your pastor. He talked with your wife and prayed with her before they took her in the ambulance. He said he would get in touch with her mother and father. They may be on the way to the hospital as we speak.

MR. KISER. While I was waiting for you to come up from the shop, I called your father. You know he and I are good friends. I let him know that Pat and his granddaughter were in an accident. He was going to go home and get his wife and go to the hospital.

I think it would be best if you did not drive right now. I will take you down to the hospital. I will have Jim follow us in your car and leave your car at the hospital.

TROOPER BROWN. I will be getting some additional information from the driver to follow up on the accident and what took place. I will be in touch with you, probably at the hospital. I'm assuming that you will be there for a number of hours until you know how your family is doing.

I will contact you either at the hospital or at home.

When we arrived at the hospital, the pastor, my parents, and Pat's parents were already there. They were all in a waiting room. The pastor led us all in a prayer for God's will to be done in each of our lives and the lives of our loved ones and in the lives of the two boys that were saved. We praised the Lord that other families did not have to deal with the loss of their young boys. We asked that God would, in time, show us the reasons or the purpose and to understand why this has been brought upon us and our loved ones. We all agreed to trust the Lord and wait, watch, and see how he works it out through our lives.

After getting a report from the doctors, I knew that my wife was expected to live. They did not know the extent of her injuries or prognosis of how long she would be healing.

It was agreed that I and my parents would go to my daughter. Pat's mother and dad would stay there with their daughter. The fate of my daughter was unknown. We had no information except that she had been flown to the trauma center at Children's Hospital.

40
The Loss

We arrived at Children's Hospital about eight hours after the accident. Going into the room, we found Surely in bed with a halo attached to her. (A halo is a medical device used to stabilize the cervical spine after traumatic injuries to the neck. The apparatus consists of a halo vest, stabilization bars, and a metal ring encircling the patient's head and fixated to the skull with multiple pins.) Surely was semiconscious. We assumed that she had been sedated. She also had an oxygen tube inserted into her nose and down her throat to keep her airways open.

A few minutes later, the doctor came into the room. He confirmed that I was her father, knowing that her mother was also in the hospital because of the accident. The doctor was introduced to the grandparents.

DOCTOR. At this point, there are still some tests that need to come back and some other tests to confirm her total condition. Apparently during the accident, her shoulder seatbelt had acted as a fulcrum on her neck in the area for the larynx. When her head was snapped, that did damage to her larynx. We don't know the full extent of the damage to the larynx, vocal cords, the neck, and the spine at this point in time. She has a few bruises and bumps on other parts of her body but seems to be overall quite healthy. She may have hit her head. We are testing for a mild concussion.

One of the puzzling things we haven't been able to figure out yet. It was noted by the emergency personnel during her flight here that two different times, they thought they heard her whistle. We have never had this happen before. We don't know if she has a broken jaw, maybe her sinuses have been damaged, or what has caused her to whistle at least two times that we know of. We are doing some additional tests to see what caused this condition.

BRUCE. I can tell you what caused that.

DOCTOR. Are you a doctor?

BRUCE. No, sir, I am not. But I know my daughter. We use signs quite often at our house. One of the signs for help or I need something is to give a loud whistle. I learned that from my wife many years ago. It is one of the signs that my daughter uses when she is down back at the spot, a fair distance from the house. You really couldn't hear somebody yell, but you could hear a whistle. I am quite sure, consciously or unconsciously, she was calling for my help.

DOCTOR. That would explain a lot. Since some of the tests have been taken, we continue to wait and see the results. I'm willing to bet that you are totally correct.

Our team is evaluating the cervical spine area. We know the spine has not been severed, and that she has feeling in her feet and toes. We know there was a major amount of damage done in the neck area. We feel that there's a high possibility that we will have to do cervical spine surgery. When operating on the cervical section of the spine (the end closest to the neck), some procedures access the spine from the front of the neck. This approach requires the surgeon to move and put traction on the laryngeal nerves in order to gain access to the spine. Hoarseness after any of these surgeries may be temporary or permanent due to vocal fold immobility.

Our fear is that the damage that has already been done may leave your daughter without a voice, being able to speak, or being able to speak over a whisper. This is a very high possibility that we evaluate at this time.

The alternative is the possibility of being paralyzed from the chest down at some later time or extreme pain throughout the balance of her life. Loss of one's voice is better than either of these two alternatives. We have to have the parents' consent in order to do cervical spine surgery. That is why I'm giving you a heads up so you can bring this to the family for a decision.

I don't mean to worry you or put you under undue stress, but it is a very, very real possibility that she will lose most of her speaking ability. At this point, we see no choice but to do the surgery.

We know it can be very, very hard on a person not to be able to communicate or speak to make their voice heard. For a young person, it sometimes makes them feel that their life is over and that they will never have a full life. There are different ways of communicating, writing of course, but also sign language. She can learn what allows people to communicate.

Too bad that your signing did not involve learning American sign language because it would help greatly in her overcoming the loss of her voice. Again, we feel at this point there is a very high possibility of her losing her voice.

BRUCE. We have a very strong faith that our Lord and Savior will prepare a way for us. He did spare her life.

We do know sign language, and we have used it for many years. Maybe this is why we have learned it. We'll wait and see what our heavenly Father has planned and praise Him that she is still alive.

41

Nine-Month Baby

The next day, we got to talk with my daughter. We explained to her what we knew about the accident, what had taken place in the accident, and how she got hurt. We explained to her the possibilities of what was going to be taking place as she started to heal. No decision would be made as far as a treatment until all the swelling had gone down in the damaged area and all the tests have come back for the doctors to review.

Surely wanted to know her mother's condition. All we could tell her was that she was alive. It was decided that my father and I would go back home to my wife so we would know her exact condition.

Arriving back home at my wife's room in the hospital, we found she was heavily sedated. Her mother and dad explained to us that when the back of the truck slammed into the side of the car, causing it to flip, the truck had hit right on the driver's door. Because Pat was the one driving, apparently that was why most of the injures are to her hip, back, and upper leg. As soon as she was stable and the swelling had gone down, they would be doing surgery.

Pat would be in the hospital for an extended period of time in traction while the leg, back, and hip were evaluated and had a chance to heal. Pat's parents also indicated that the doctors were very concerned whether she would be able to walk again. At this time, they were hoping that she would be able to. Thinking it would be a long and hard recovery over a matter of years, not months or weeks, before she might be able to walk on her own, there would be a lengthy hospital stay and a lengthy recovery with a lot of rehab treatments.

DAD. Son, we need to talk. Let's step into the room here so we can be by ourselves.

This is not a pep talk. The reality is there is evil in this world and there are circumstances that happen to each of us that are not exactly what we would choose or what we would want. I know right now you're questioning why, why did this happen to my lovely wife and my lovely daughter. Why is not the question we should be asking. We should be thanking the Lord for the things that we do have, not those things that we don't have. We still have both of our loved ones with us. This is the time to be patient, to wait, and watch to see what God is working out for all our lives.

It is written in the scriptures, "Behold, the virgin shall conceive and bear a son." (Isaiah 7:14, RSV) Mary conceived and gave birth to Jesus. Mary was pregnant for nine months. Jesus was a nine-month baby. Jesus had to wait thirty years before He could start His ministry.

I don't think it's going to be as little as nine months before we see the full results of Surely and Pat's healing. I don't think it's going to be as long as thirty years either. Meanwhile we take one day at a time, praise the Lord for what we have, and watch to see how He works this all out in our lives, for His glory and for our benefit. You have seen him work in our lives before. Watch and see him work in all of our lives again now.

Now we are going to go get something to eat which is something you have not done in the last day and a half. I buy, you eat, got it?

42
Wonder

After getting something to eat, we returned back to the hospital, where I was going to spend the night with my wife.

DAD. Son, I talked with your mother. Surely's surgery is scheduled for the day after tomorrow in the morning. We should go home and get some rest. We should be going back to be with your daughter tomorrow afternoon.

　　(Having food in my stomach, the adrenaline had worn off. I did get very tired.)

PAT. Your father is right. Both of you need to get some rest. My parents will be back in a little while, and they will spend the night with me. My surgery isn't supposed to start till seven tomorrow morning. You can be back here and see me before I go in for surgery. I should be out of surgery and recovery by noon. I will be okay.

Love you. Get your tired ugly face out of here and go home. Get a good night's rest so you can go safely to be with our daughter. Keep in touch and let me know what's going on with her. Now, get out of my room.

Her tone as she spoke was such that I didn't want to argue with her. She was right. I did need some rest. I took her, I'll say, advice.

After Pat was out of surgery and we had a chance to talk with the doctors, we made a beeline toward Children's Hospital to be with Surely. I was impatient and wanted to see my daughter. I wanted to know that she was doing well.

My father-in-law was staying with his daughter. My mother-in-law came along with us to be with my mother while Surely was having surgery.

We were about forty-five minutes from Children's Hospital when there was a piece of debris lying in the road. I ran over it and ruined one tire. We had to stop and change the tire. My dad knew that I was very frustrated.

DAD. Son, what would your mother say to you now if she was here?

BRUCE. I don't want another life lesson.

DAD. What would your mother say to you if she was here?

BRUCE. Something like haste makes waste or patience is a virtue. You would say wait and see what God is doing to protect you from something or working at trying to help me. This is a waste of time. I have to change the tire.

Nothing was said by any of us when, twenty minutes later, we came upon an accident. A truck had gone through an intersection and smashed into a car. I will always wonder if that could have been us if it had not been for the flat tire. It seems like I can still get it wrong most of the time, but I'm trying the best I can do.

43
Squealed

We arrived at Children's Hospital in plenty of time to talk to Surely. We shared with her that her mother was through surgery and was doing as well as could be expected.

Surely was told by the doctors that, with the airway tube still in, she was not even to try to talk. She signed us that she was doing fine, and she wanted to go see her mother. The doctors had told her that it would be probably three to five days after her surgery before she would be able to go home. She thought that was way too long. She wanted to go now.

BRUCE. Surely, you know you will be home before your mother. You will get to see her in the hospital.

I did not speak about the fact that I had just got a life lesson on being patience. Some things in life take a reasonable amount of time. Healing is one you should not hurry, or you may do more harm than good.

I hope I have learned to be patient because the scripture says that tribulation brings patience or teaches patience. I've had enough tribulation over the last few days. Hopefully I've learned to be patient. I have been very good at being wrong before and probably will be again.

A nurse came and took Surely to prep her for surgery, leaving us alone.

BRUCE. Mother, I would like to update you on Pat's physical condition and the doctors' prognosis on her continuing treatment now that Surely is not here.

The long-term prognosis is very good. She will be able to totally recover or at least 90 percent. Her back is not broken, a lot of ligaments are separated or torn loose from the bones. They did have to put pins or plates in to support her hip and her leg. The leg was a special type of break. It was spun or twisted rather than a straight fracture. They figure that she'll have to have at least two more surgeries, and that they will have to be done over the next year.

Rehabilitation may take anywhere from two to five years, depending on how she handles the surgeries and how active she can be during the rehabilitation and recuperation. She came very close to dying because of the amount of damage that was done. So far, she is recuperating and tolerating the treatment quite well.

Mother, you would say her guardian angel did a lot of work in keeping her alive and doing a good job protecting as he did.

MOTHER. Bruce, what were you thinking? You should not have been speeding. You should know if you are trusting your father. You do not need to be impatient, rushing, or hurrying. You should not be speeding. Going slower, you would have been able to see the piece of debris on the road and avoided hitting it. That could have caused a major accident by blowing out a tire or losing control the car. If you had slowed down, you might have been able to see what was in the road.

BRUCE. Thanks, Dad. I think we were talking about Pat's condition, injuries, and treatment.

DAD. Don't blame me. I haven't had a chance to talk to your mother in private yet.

BRUCE. Well, that only leaves one other person that could have squealed on me.

MOTHER. Don't blame Barbara. She is as concerned as I am about our family and what's going on right now. We all are concerned about both families and getting through this together.

BRUCE. You are right. Barbara and Dad have already spoken up in your place in the car. I think none of us have been eating like we should. I, for one, am hungry.

I know you, Mother, haven't been eating like you should. I bet you have not been away from Surely's side from the time you got here. Come on, Dad will buy us something to eat. Right, Dad?

DAD. Right.

44
Incorrect

After Surely's surgery, the doctor came out and talked with us. Everything had gone well with the surgery on the neck. But it was their belief that there was permanent damage done to her larynx. She probably would never be able to speak again in a full voice.

We decided it would be better not to tell her of our concerns, but tell her it is very, very important that she not talk, or try to talk, until the neck brace was totally removed in a number of weeks when she went back. Let her realize the loss of her voice over time on her own, and emotionally, she would be better able to handle the loss. Let her know it would probably be five or six days before she would be able to go home. She would wear the neck brace and was not to take it off other than to wash her neck. No showers at least for the first three weeks, then she would be going back for a checkup.

Dad and I were there six days later to take Surely home. As we were getting in the car:

SURELY, **signing.** Will you let Grandpa drive?

BRUCE. Why let Grandpa drive?

SURELY, **signing.** I want you to sit in the back with me so we can talk.

BRUCE. I can talk and drive at the same time. Did somebody say something about my driving when I came to see you?

SURELY, **signing.** No. You may be able to drive and talk, but you can't drive and watch me sign things to you at the same time and be safe. I want Grandpa to drive so that we can talk, or you can watch me sign.

BRUCE. You are right, I cannot drive safely watching you sign. Again, I get it wrong. I'll let Grandpa drive. Dad will you drive, please?

DAD. Bruce I don't like it when you say you got it wrong. That's a negative response to things. Shouldn't you try to change that to a more positive response?

BRUCE. Okay, I guess you are right. I don't know exactly how to say you're right without saying I got it wrong. How about I'm right about not getting it correct, would that make you happier?

DAD. It's a start.

BRUCE. I know there are a couple places we can stop and get ice cream on the way home. I surely know Surely loved ice cream before the surgery. I think you probably still do.

SURELY, **signing.** Yes.

BRUCE. Surely can buy us ice cream now that we have sprung her out of the hospital. Right?

SURELY. (A look of disapproval. She hits me on the arm.)

BRUCE. Well, I guess I'm right about getting it incorrect again? Surely, you know you are your mother's daughter.

DAD. Keep it up, Surely. You're better at keeping him in line than I ever have been.

BRUCE. I thank God that I get to take my angel home without her halo. (Closing her in a tight loving hug, giving her a kiss.) Let's go get ice cream and go see your mother.

45
White House

As we got in the car and headed out of the parking lot:

SURELY, signing, asking questions specifically about her mother. What is her condition? What was the surgery for? What is the prognosis? What is the amount of time it will take for her to heal? What can I do to help? When can she come home?

BRUCE. Whoa. Whoa. Slow down. I'm not as good at reading signs as your mother is. I'm not getting all of what you're trying to ask. You're going to have to tolerate my inability to sign, as well as you and your mother.

I got it that you want to know about your mother's condition. When she was in the emergency room, they put her leg in traction, holding it in place until surgery. Surgery was done on her hip and her leg. Restraints and braces were put in for her back. Last we knew, she's going to have at least two more surgeries sometime within the next year or so. She will probably be two to five years in rehab before we can get her muscles and their strength back from the damage that was done in the accident.

Once she gets out of traction and out of the cast, she will be in a wheelchair during rehabilitation till she can walk.

SURELY, **signing.** What about the boys on the bikes? Did they get killed? Did they die? Did they get hurt? How bad? Who were they or who are they?

BRUCE. We don't know who they were or are. Their names were not released because they are juveniles. The hospital would not tell us if they came in or if they didn't. We know nothing about them. Officer Brown did indicate there were two boys on bikes that jetted into the road in front of the truck. We heard that one may have hurt his leg. That's all we know about the boys.

SURELY, *signing*. If the boys are alive, God must have wanted to save them for some reason. Even if it cost me my voice, it's worth it, because my Savior gave up His life for me. I'm willing to give up my voice for somebody's life. I just hope they realize the gift they've been given. I know about my voice and the possibilities of never being able to speak again. I can see it in your faces and the concern of the doctors.

BRUCE. Dad, later I will tell you what we have been talking about. I know you've only heard one side of the conversation. I want you to know what a remarkable young lady that you have as a granddaughter and how proud I am of her.

DAD. Hope you guys are still hungry. I Scream for Mustard Ice Cream restaurant is coming up shortly, and I'm stopping and getting a burger and ice cream. Are you two ready to eat?

*****

The Cow Palace Farm was known in a wide area for their unusual taste of ice cream. Featuring every two weeks a different ice cream, such as spaghetti, mustard, ketchup, pizza, horseradish, pumpkin, candy cane, fireball, licorice, pot roast, lasagna, cabbage, brussels sprouts. You never knew what they were going to have for flavors of ice cream.

They also had all the flavors that were standby: chocolate, vanilla, butter pecan, black cherry, White House etc., etc. They always had one strange flavored featured in their name: I Scream For? Ice Cream.

The Cow Palace Farms raised all their own beef, and it was sold in the restaurant. They are known for their different flavored ice creams, their good beef, and their flavored milks.

SURELY, **signing.** I haven't found a kind of ice cream yet that I don't like. Do I get to try all of them to see if there's one I don't like?

BRUCE. Only if you don't want to see your mother today.

DAD. I know you guys are talking about trying all the flavors of ice cream, but you're
limited to three kinds today.

BRUCE. But, Dad, Surely is still recuperating
from her injuries.

SURELY. (Smiles at her dad and winks.)

46
Would Not

We arrived back at the hospital to see Pat. After some time, it was getting late in the evening.

BRUCE. Surely, we need to go home so that you can get your rest. I know you want to spend more time with your mother but there's going to be a lot more time that you'll be able to spend with her in the hospital.

The next day, which was Friday, we came to the hospital. Surely insisted that she stay with her mother that night and tomorrow and possibly even Sunday. There was no objection. Surely's grandparents needed to go home and get some rest also from the stress of being in the hospital all the time.

On Saturday, there were a number of visitors that came to see Pat. Two, Tony and Leroy, stated they were there to see Pat. Tony came first, then about two hours later, Leroy stopped in, supposedly to see Pat. It's good that they came to see, I will say Pat, because they did not understand sign language, and Surely could not talk. Pat needed to translate or interpret what was being signed by Surely. I told Pat later that both boys had called and wanted to talk to Surely. I had indicated that she was spending time at the hospital with her mother, and she would not talk to them, but they could go see Pat. I think they went to see Pat because Surely was there.

Pat informed all the visitors that Surely's vocal cords have been damaged, and she was not to try to talk. Surely could sign and that Pat would translate for her. Pat told me later it was a very interesting situation. The boys really seemed to want to say other things, but because she was translating for Surely, they were very cautious of what they asked or said. Surely, at the same time, was very guarded in her responses. Needless to say, it was an interesting time.

I could have had a lot more fun and entertainment if I had been the one interpreting for Surely. But Pat was the one there and would only translate specifically what was signed.

47
Trojan Horse

Sunday afternoon, I went from church to see my wife and daughter. There were numerous get-well cards for a speedy recovery for my wife and my daughter. Some members of the congregation wanted to know what they could do to be of service during my wife's recovery.

I was informed that Pat and Surely had a plan of action to take care of us till both of them had fully recovered.

Surely did not want to go back to school after realizing on Saturday that she could not communicate with her classmates.

Pat was going to need help during her recovery, and Surely desperately wanted to be the one to help her mother in being able to get around.

First, I was to contact the school and let them know that Surely was going to be homeschooled for the balance of her junior and senior year. That I did.

Second, I was to take Surely to get her a car so she would be able to get around and take her mother to appointments. During therapy and rehab, people would help get Pat in and out of the car.

Surely would do the housekeeping and some cooking with her mother's help. Pat would be the homeschool teacher for Surely.

I took Surely to find a car. She found a minivan. It was black and had tinted windows all the way around except for the driver's window and windshield. That was the one she liked. We agreed that her mother should be able to get in and out of the van fairly easily in time.

BRUCE. Are you sure you want this van? It's black, looks like a big rock, or should I say a piece of slate. Wouldn't you rather have a brighter color such as red, blue, green, or even white?

SURELY, **signing.** No. I want that one. I am going to call it my Trojan Horse.

BRUCE. Why are you going to call it your Trojan Horse?

SURELY, **signing.** Horses are one of the ways that people get around. Trojan is from the story of the Trojan Horse, where the important things were unseen inside and could not be seen by people outside.

After hearing her reasons, I was fearful that she may be starting to withdraw from people, keeping her emotions and thoughts and fears all within herself. The doctors had warned us that getting used to not being able to fully communicate with other people sometimes is a very hard thing to overcome.

From birth, she was one of the most talk-ative people that I knew. In school, she was known for giving very long verbal reports.

SURELY, **signing.** Dad, I would like you to do one thing for me, but don't tell Mom about it, please.

Bruce. What is it and why don't you want your mother to know?

Surely, **signing.** I want you to get me a truck-load of sand.

Bruce. Did I understand you correctly? You want me to get you a truckload of sand?

Surely, **signing.** Yes. I want you to get me a truckload of sand and dump it by the pathway down to the spot. I want to make a walkway of the slates that are piled out back so I can get my mother in her wheelchair down back to the garden area. I don't want her to know about it until the walkway is done. I need the sand to fill in around the slates.

Bruce. Tell me when you want it, and I will see that there's a truckload of sand there for you to use.

48
Ice Broken

Some seven weeks after the accident, the two grandfathers, myself, and Surely returned to the hospital for her doctor's appointment, hopefully to get the neck collar taken off permanently.

Luckily, the doctors never had to give her one of the cone collars like they put on dogs to keep them from biting or chewing. There had been some comments made to her that if her doctor had been a veterinarian, she would have had a cone collar and not just the collar. Surely would snarl but she was not able to growl. It was kind of a light spirited fun way of dealing with her affliction with her neck and not being able to speak.

DAD. I see I Scream for Bacon Ice Cream. Are we going to stop now or on our way back?

SURELY, **signing**. Both.

BRUCE. Surely signed both.

MR. HAWTHORNE. Well, I could go for a burger.

BRUCE. It's settled then. We'll stop now and on the way home.

*****

The doctor checked Surely's neck and talked with her about pain and discomfort.

DOCTOR. How are you doing?

SURELY, **signing**. I am doing fine.

DOCTOR. I know the collar did not stop you from trying to talk. You didn't try too hard, did you?

SURELY, **signing**. No. Tried a little.

DOCTOR. What were the results?

SURELY, **signing**. I can't talk.

DOCTOR. We were afraid that you would lose your voice. Even now, this doesn't mean that, at some point, some of your voice will not come back. You still have a lot of healing to do over a long time. Try not to talk. I would like to see you again in six months when we will evaluate you again.

*****

It was a very solemn ride home.

SURELY, **signing.** Did you come to be depressed with me, or did you come for the ice cream? I think you came for the ice cream. I surely did not come just to see a doctor. We agreed we were going to stop on the way back.

BRUCE. Let's try something new. I think I'm going to try the strawberry rhubarb that's the special they have advertised on the sign for this week.

You might say the ice was broken by ice cream, but actually it was the accep-tance of reality at this point in Surely's life.

49
Quiet

Just a few minutes before arriving back home, Surely signed:

Surely. Dad, I want to have a cookout down at the spot with my friends from school. School has been out a couple weeks. Most of my friends know I can't talk. I would like them to know that I'm okay. I would like to invite them for cookout. Is that okay with you?

Bruce. Yes. I would be happy to pay for the food. You go ahead and set it up with your friends, or do you want me to contact them?

Surely. No. I will write them and let them know the time and place of the cookout I'm having and would like them to come in two weeks or Saturday after next. Would that be okay?

Bruce. Okay. If you want my help, you'll need to ask for it.

Shirley, signing. Understood.

*****

Tuesday, after Surely's party, I was asked to come down and see Mr. Kiser in his office.

Mr. Kiser. Bruce, we need to talk. Please have a seat. There are some things I want to let you know. They're not all bad. They're not all good. We'll have to wait and see how things work out to determine good or bad.

First, we are going to have to lay off Pat. Her sick pay has run out. I don't want to just fire her or furlough her. I will lay her off, and she'll be able to get unemployment. I hope it won't be too much of a financial burden, but at this point, I don't have a lot of other choices.

Something else that I don't have a lot of choice in and I don't know how it's going to work out is that I've been informed by the owners of the hotel that they are considering selling out to a franchise chain. This is only in the investigation part for now. Apparently, they are interested in getting out of the hotel business.

What I plan to do is change your job title and make you head of purchasing and maintenance. It will be more work with no increase in pay. Hopefully it will position you, so if the hotel is sold, they would choose to keep you on because of your skills. I have no idea if I will still be here or not. All I know is at this point, they're are looking into a lot of options and changing ownership of the hotel.

Please don't say anything to anybody about this conversation since I was asked to keep it as quiet as possible. I consider you as family, and I want to do what I can to protect and help your family. I don't think you have to worry at this time. It will probably be a year, maybe two years, before this all comes down. But I want you to have those positions now so that you have a history of doing the job. Do you understand?

Bruce. Yes. Thank you. We will pray to see God's will work out for you and us to His glory.

Mr. Kiser. When you say we, I believe you mean you and your wife. I would ask that you only let her know that she has been laid off and will be able to get unemployment. She doesn't need the worry or be concerned about you losing a job. I would like to keep this as low profile as possible.

50
Jericho

I was at home building a small ramp in to the house when Surely came home.

SURELY, whistling. Stop or Where are you?

BRUCE, whistling. I'm here or come here.

I'm glad you're back. Guess what your mother is getting for her birthday?

SURELY, **signing**. A ramp to come up three steps?

BRUCE. No. Silly girl. The ramp is for you to help you get your mother up into the house and down out of the house to therapy.

SURELY, **signing**. What is she getting for her birthday?

BRUCE. I talked with your mother earlier. The doctors told her she'll be able to come home. It's going to be on her birthday. I need the ramp to be done by then. I got two days. I should be able to have it done by Friday.

SURELY, **signing**. I need the truckload of sand and eight railroad ties.

BRUCE. Railroad ties?

SURELY, **signing**. Yes. Mother and I discussed this the other day. Being we didn't get to plant a garden this summer, we could make an asparagus bed. Asparagus is one of the plants you've got to really be patient with. It takes two to three years for the asparagus bed to produce asparagus. Mother said asparagus would be good for you. I didn't know you liked asparagus.

BRUCE. I don't dislike asparagus. I think your mother was trying to tell me that I still need to learn to be a little more patient. Why do you need the railroad ties?

SURELY, **signing**. We are going to make an asparagus bed, and you need ties in order to build the bed up above ground level.

BRUCE. Who is "we"? Your mother will not be able to get her chair down to the garden.

Surely, **signing**. Tony, Leroy, Joshua, and myself.

Bruce. Who is Joshua?

Shirley, **signing**. When we had the party the other week, I asked for some help with planning the slate walk and making the asparagus bed.

Bruce. Who is Joshua? I know you can hear me because it's your speech you have the problem with, not hearing.

Surely, **signing**. Asparagus is one of the first plants that greets us in springtime. It's a perennial, which means that once it gets established, asparagus will return year after year.

Bruce. Who is Joshua?

Surely, **signing**. I am trying to tell you about asparagus. We are going to start with planting seeds. Plants may take two to three years to truly get started and produce so patience is needed.

Bruce. I am patiently waiting to know who Joshua is, and you are trying not to talk about Joshua.

SURELY, **signing.** If you would read your Bible, you would know that Joshua is the one that led the Israelites around the city of Jericho until the walls fell down, and they conquered the city in the Holy Land.

But then again, asparagus is one of those plants that what is not seen is more important than what is seen. It doesn't like to get its feet wet or to be in wet soil. They have a lot of roots.

BRUCE. I am waiting.

SURELY, **signing.** The plant can be productive for up to twenty-five years, so we think it's worth the wait. Asparagus has male and female plants. Male plants produce the most sprouts, and the female plants produces berries. This is where we get the seeds. Regions with cool winters are best for this cool-season crop, which comes up in early spring.

BRUCE. Have you told me everything that you know about asparagus?

SURELY, **signing.** No. I know a lot more.

BRUCE. You've told me more than I need to know about asparagus. I need to know about Joshua. I know about the one in the Bible. I read the Bible every day. I want to know about the Joshua that's going to be here with you and helping in the garden.

SURELY, **signing.** Surely you know who Josh is. He's a tall good-looking young man with dark hair and green eyes. Is funny and has a great smile. He sits up front in church with the teens every Sunday. He was on the debate team with me.

Josh is the one that I was going with to the junior senior prom. He was a senior and graduated last year and is going to go here to the community college next year.

He wants to learn sign language. He wants me to teach him, so when we debate, he will be able to tell if he is winning the debate against me.

BRUCE. Oooh, him. (Why am I the last to know? I still don't know him.)

SURELY, **signing.** I'll need more sand than what I planned on for just the walkway. We will be digging up the sod and soil of the

slate way path then mixing it with the sand to make the beds for the asparagus.
If I could get ten railroad ties, we could have a white asparagus bed also. Do you think we could do that?

BRUCE. You have it all planned out. I will get ten railroad ties and the sand.

SURELY, **signing.** I want mother to think when we're working down back, we're working on the asparagus bed. She won't know about the slate walk we are planning for her to be able get down to the spot and the garden.

51
Artist

Pat's therapy was scheduled for three times a week. After the second week, she was in so much pain and discomfort that the therapy was cut back to two times a week. That was less intense. Pat needed to gain some strength before they could do the last surgery. Hopefully, to be scheduled in the middle of November.

About the first of October when Surely and Pat were on their way for a therapy session:

PAT. Surely, I want to know what's going on down at the spot. I know in August, a couple of the weekends, that you had some of your classmates over and you were working, building asparagus beds. I also know that asparagus beds need to have porous soil, which means that's why you were using the sand, but where did you get the other soil to mix with it to make it porous and still be able to hold moisture?

I know Josh is coming over, supposedly only because you're teaching him sign. Tony is still coming over, and you're still working on the slate art. Leroy has been coming over, but it's too late in the year to be working on the garden.

I'm not as good at figuring things out as your father. By the way, he's been acting very dumb about the whole situation and doesn't have anything to say or do with what you're up to. He said you don't confide in him about the planning for the spot or the garden.

I will tell you what I think about what I see and where you're working down back. I think you dug up the sod in the path going down back, and that's what you used with the sand to make the asparagus beds. Now you're planning to use the slate to make a slate walkway. Am I right or wrong?

SURELY, **signing**. Right.

PAT. What's the big secret then? Why is your dad so quiet about what's going on?

SURELY, **signing**. Dad doesn't know all the details of what I've got planned. I asked him not to say anything because I wanted it to be a surprise when you were able to come back down to the garden in your wheelchair or to be able to walk down when you got better. I asked Dad not to handle any of the slates or move them, but he doesn't know why.

PAT. Would you like to tell me more about your plans? I would like to know what you got planned.

SURELY, **signing**. Surely, you know I love you and Dad. I'm so sorry that you got hurt in the accident. I enjoy so much working in the garden with you. My art teacher told me years ago that I had the skill of an artist. I want to use my skill as an artist.

You told me in the hospital that just saying something does not make it true, and many times, actions speak louder than words like when you held my hand as I was crying in your hospital room about not being able to speak.

I want to put into slate those things that I cannot say. I'm the only one knowing all the plans. Part of the plan is a picture story in slate of our family's love of the spot and the garden.

I'm going to make the path out of the slate. The slates will have pictures that have to do with our lives at the spot and the garden, both human, animals, and plants.

I cannot tell you verbally that I love you anymore. I know you would like to be able to come down to the garden and be with me. I want it to be easy for you to get to the garden. The path will be to honor you and Dad and anyone that has helped or been part of the garden or the spot.

I think I'm going to name it the Unspoken Garden.

52
Monkeys

After Pat's surgery, the first part of November life became a little more routine. Surely doing her schooling with Pat, taking Pat to her therapy, me going to work.

Routine does not always mean boring as our lives never seem to be boring. The first of April is known as April Fool's Day. We all know we get to do a few crazy things and try to pull April fool's jokes on people.

Both Tony and Leroy showed up at the house at the same time after school and wanted to talk with Surely. Surely was not home at the time. She had gone to the store for her mother.

PAT. Surely should return home shortly.

I know all this because Pat told me what took place. Otherwise, I would have been clueless, as I am most of the time, where women are concerned and what they are doing and why.

Pat relayed to me that while the boys were waiting, Tony and Leroy were discussing the April Fool's dance at the school and which one would get to ask Surely to go with him to the dance. It was decided that both would ask Surely. Surely would make the decision of which one would go with her to the dance.

The important thing about the dance was it was to be a costume dance, preferably going dressed up as a court jester, clown, or some other off-the-wall interesting character, real or fiction.

Upon Surely's return home, Pat signed the information she had gleaned from the boys talking about the dance and their intentions to ask her to go to the dance with them.

Pat acted as interpreter again. The boys had not become real efficient at sign language, and it was easier than Surely writing everything out in response to their questions.

It was decided that Surely would not make a decision at that time until she had a chance to talk with Josh.

SURELY, **signing.** Both of you would be happy
    and content if not pleased with my deci-
    sion. I need you to come back the Monday
    night before the dance. The dance is two
    Saturdays away. Okay?
TONY. Yes.
LEROY. Yes.

As I said, life may become routine with going to school or work, but that doesn't mean it's boring. At this point, I was clueless how Surely was going to work this out. As you know, I am good about getting it right about being incorrect, which I did not want to do again, so I was willing to wait and watch and see what took place.

Surely had contacted Josh with a typing synthetic voice machine provided through the phone company. He informed her that he would not be able to go with her. He is in a study group that would be studying for a very important test coming up next Monday.

Pat and Surely spend a lot of time in Pat's craft room over the next week. I had no idea what they were planning.

Monday, when Tony and Leroy showed up as requested, they were told that they both have the opportunity to go to the dance but not as themselves but as one of the trio of monkeys. (No. Not the musical group The Monkeys. You would need four monkeys for that, and Josh was not able to go to the dance.) The trio group would go as speak no evil, see no evil, and hear no evil. Surely would be going as the speak no evil monkey.

SURELY, **signing.** Do you want to take the other two places?

Both boys jumped at the opportunity to be part of the trio, which was a good choice because they won first place in the costume contest at the dance.

53

Construction

April 15 is a day that I will remember for a long time. No, not because the fishing season started then. Starting of fishing is one of the three big days of business at the hotel when we are usually full to capacity. The last Monday in November is one of those days also being the first day of deer hunting season in your state, and a lot of out of state hunters come to town that weekend.

The third time is fair week. It is when we are usually full to capacity at the hotel because of people coming back in town to go to the local county fair to compete in one or many of the activities and meet family and friends. It is a hometown week with a lot of good fair food, a lot of good hometown food sold at the local charity booths, such as fresh homemade pie, cinnamon rolls and sticky buns, two foot long subs made with homemade bread, hot sausage sandwiches, baked potatoes with real butter, and all the toppings you might want. As you can tell, I go for the food.

There are two reasons why I will remember that day. The first is that is the day we met with the doctors, and they said Pat is making a full recovery. She will not need any more surgeries that they could foresee at that point.

Pat could start walking a little at a time with a walker instead of staying in the wheelchair. Pat was to use the walker till she could walk or stand for a minimum of fifteen minutes at one time before not using the walker anymore. I expect it will be forty to sixty days before she will be able to accomplish that. "Do not rush it" was the doctor's order.

PAT. Doctor, could you make that an order that I am to stay in the wheelchair when there are other people around so that they don't trip me and I fall? That way, I can still be waited on hand and foot.

DOCTOR. That is a little late now. Your husband already heard me say that you would be able to get around without the wheel-chair. Besides I know Bruce. He's more than willing to do whatever you would ask of him. I think you're going to enjoy the freedom of being able to get around on your own once again. Don't rush it.

The second reason I will remember that day is what corresponded in Mr. Kiser's office. I was called into Mister Kiser's office. He informed me he had met with the three private investors, who were thinking of buy-ing the hotel and building another hotel in town. They had done some explorer studies and thought it was well feasible to have two or three hotels in a town this size. The most important part was that they had no inter-est in managing the hotels.

They had asked Mr. Kiser to not seek other employment but stay on to manage all the hotels, placing in the positions those people that he thought would do a good job for them. They had approved his choice of keeping me on as purchasing and maintenance manager. I would get a little increase of pay as work on the new places started and a big increase in the contract when they are operating.

They had to acquire some land. Depending on the price of the land, they may need to acquire a little more funding. The three of them each had his own construction company. The building of the hotels was not going to be a problem. They expected that within a year and nine months to two years, the other hotels would be built and operational.

Mr. Kiser also asked when Pat would be able to come back to work. Her position would be open for her as soon as she was able to do the job. I thanked him for all that he had done for my family and was doing for my family. His letting me know this took a lot stress off me, knowing that I had a job.

54

Louder than Words

I know from somebody much smarter than I am that for every action, there is a reaction. I did not expect the reaction I got from my wife and daughter, knowing Pat was going to be able to go down to the garden.

I should have known I was about to lose the other half of my two-car garage. Oooh, I didn't mean that it disappeared, and I didn't mean it was damaged or destroyed. I just meant that the other side became a greenhouse, and one half has been an artist's workshop for the last two years. I now have a no car garage because my wife will be working in her new greenhouse. There still is a lot more to do in the garden because the garage still has a lot of plants that need to be planted in the garden.

SURELY, **signing.** I want to have a party for you the Saturday before Mother's Day. (Mother's Day is always the second Sunday in May)

Mom, please don't go down to the garden for now. Please wait till the party. I know the party is for you, but would you like to make up the menu and cook the food or part of the food, or would you rather I have it catered? I could order pizza wings and salad.

PAT. You know I want to do the food, and one thing we will have is hotdogs.

SURELY. I invited family and some friends from the church. I also asked Tony, Leroy, Josh, and a couple of my girlfriends that helped me to invite your friends down to see the Unspoken Garden path the Saturday of the party. I wanted family, friends, and the boys that helped with the Unspoken Garden path and patio there to celebrate your return to the garden spot. Hopefully it will bring back memories of some good times.

That Saturday, we had the party to christen the Unspoken Garden path.

There were about seventy people that showed up, all well-wishers for Pat. Most, if not all, eagerly wanted to see the artwork in the Unspoken Garden.

The helpers on the garden told people about seeing the plants' unique artwork, and somehow the local paper found out about the Unspoken Garden path. There was a little article in the paper under true stores dealing with Mother's Day. "Local Artist Honors Mother by Making Unspoken Garden Path. Let your mother know you love her even if you can't say it in words. Remember actions sometimes speak louder than words. Show her you love her by your actions."

55

For Sale

The day after the article was in the paper, I came home and there was a car in the driveway. I could see a person at the spot. I walked down to see what he was doing. He was bent over and pulling one of the tiles up from of the edge of the patio.

BRUCE. Hey. Stop. Stop, thief.

What are you doing? Stop pulling that up.

Hey, I'm talking to you.

As I got about six feet away from the man, he stood up turned and looked at me.

NILES. Hi. Sorry I did not hear you coming. I am deaf so I did not know you were there till I could feel your footsteps on the ground. I do read lips so if you would please face me when you're talking to me, I will be able to understand what you're saying.

BRUCE. What are you doing? You can't just come in here and tear up a slate. They are my daughter's. They're her artwork. Leave it lay right there. I will put it back in its place.

NILES. I wasn't going to steal it. I'll buy it. I'll pay for it. I will pay well over what she thinks it may be worth. There are a couple reasons why I want and need this one. I need it to show my bosses the quality of her work.

BRUCE. They are not for sale. My daughter hasn't sold any of the slates that she's made.

NILES. I'm sorry. I'm truly sorry. I did not mean any disrespect to you or your daughter by trying to lift that slate.

Here is my card. Please call me Niles. I am the point man for Trinity Hotels. I hope you are Bruce. Mr. Kiser told me where you lived and suggested that I talk with you. As you may already know, we are planning on taking over the hotel that you now work at, and Trinity Hotels is planning on building two other hotels in this general area. We are looking for land, and we were looking for something that we can tie into as a theme or a special attraction for our hotels. The owners of the other companies are intrigued with the article they read in the paper about the Unspoken Garden.

Mr. Kiser believes that you own a fair section of land here, and you might be interested in selling some of it to Trinity Hotels for a good price. They would also like to be able to purchase Unspoken Garden Walk if they could get it to go all the way down along the creek. They know about the history of skipping stones and would like it to be part of the garden walk along the creek.

BRUCE. We are not interested at all in selling any of the land that has anything to do with the garden or the spot.

NILES. Would you please think it over? Talk it over with your wife?

Now about the slate that I was pulling up, I want that slate or one like it. It would mean a great deal to me and my family if we could acquire it. You see, the boy that is represented on that slate is my youngest brother, Timothy. He was being chased by the young man that was bullying him all the time. He wasn't paying attention to what he was doing while riding his bicycle. He was just trying to get away from the other boy. He could have been killed that day, and I know the price your family has paid for his life.

BRUCE. Niles, you go up to the house, go in the back door to the garage, find my daughter, Surely, and tell her what you just told me. Ask her if she would make you a duplicate of that slate. I don't think you'll be able to buy one. I know she won't speak to you the same as you will not hear her not speak to you. (Smiles and a slightly chuckles.)

56

Love Garden

I got a hand spade from the box of garden tools that Surely had there for planting the slates.

Kneeling down and starting to replace the slate with the boy and bicycle on it, I realized one other slate had been disturbed, so I pulled it up so I could clean it and put it back in the place Surely had it.

I heard a whistle coming from behind me. I stood up with tears running down my face. Surely was running toward me. I had uncovered my daughter's secret seeds of love she had planted of things that she could not say but felt very deeply.

Her heavenly Father knows the seeds that she was planting. God will not be mocked, what you plant you shall also reap in the fullness of time. Too many times we do not let other people know how we truly feel. That is a shame.

I knew what was wrong and why she was whistling and running to me.

SURELY, **signing**. You know, don't you? You know.

BRUCE. Yes, I know.

Etching on the back of all of them?
SURELY, **signing**. Most.

On the back of the slate of the boy on his bicycle was etched: "Surely know our heavenly Father is watching over us [a heart]. Surely."

On the back of the other was written Galatians 6:7–9, TEV. I will paraphrase it for those of you that do not know it or will not take the time to look it up. God will not be mocked, what you sow you shall reap in the fullness of time, be it physical planning of a crop for the planting of our spiritual desires. So let us do good to all people that your harvest can be good.

Surely was the only one that knew there was something on the back of the slates. Now I know and you know.

Surely has two gardens at the spot. One is a physical food garden with its fruits, vegetables, and flowers, which provide for our physical sustenance of life. The second garden is the Unspoken (Love) Garden.

Surely had engraved on the back of each slate a prayer, a request, a hope, or thanks. Surely and her heavenly Father knew what kind of seed was planted and what kind of fruit would develop in the fullness of God's timing. It's what's behind that hard outer shell that is the most important things in life not seen, like love, peace, joy, acceptance, companionship, sense of family, fellowship, prayer, worship, faith, hope.

When somebody that dies of a broken heart, their heart didn't physically break even though people do have physical heart attacks. You can kill a person quicker by taking away all hope than you can by taking away all food.

Earlier, I had wanted my dad to know what a remarkable young lady Surely is. I want you to know that also. Surely had not judged her heavenly Father's plan for her by being in a car accident or losing her voice. Surely's faith and hope were in her Savior, Jesus Christ.

Katharine Hepburn once said, "To plant a garden is to believe in tomorrow." Surely seeds of faith are planted in her love garden. I know she will be ok and in the fullness of time, she would see God's plan for her. Surely knows that farmers must dig up, till the soil, mechanics must breakdown before they can repair, watchmakers tear apart before they can repair, shoemakers have to tear apart before they can repair. Contractors must tear up and put in a good foundation in order to have a good building. Don't judge your life and give up hope. You may be in the planting season, not the harvest season.

Pat has told Surely a number of times that she was hurt, crushed, and disappointed when she did not get into culinary school, but that she is happier now than when she thought she ever could be by having Surely as her daughter, being a wife, cooking, catering, and working at the hotel.

Do not judge your life by your plans for it. Judge your life by who you are trusting in to plan your life.

57
Time to Leave

Niles followed Surely back down to the spot, not knowing why she so abruptly left him standing while talking to her. Niles did not know all that went on between her and her dad. Surely's back was to him, and he could not read sign language, but he knew that he had upset Surely and that his disturbing the stone was not a good thing.

SURELY, **signing.** I love you, Dad. It's okay you know. (Gives him a hug.)

BRUCE, **looking over Surely's shoulder.** Young man, Niles? Is that correct?

NILES. Yes.

BRUCE. Did you get to request my daughter to make a duplicate cut slate of your brother and the bike?

NILES. No. I said I had pulled up the slate of the bike, and boy and you were going to place it back for her and she ran out.

SURELY, **signing.** Why that one?

NILES. I believe, by how it was placed, that it represented the boy that caused the accident that you and your mother were hurt in. It was along the edge. I thought it could be replaced easily. I wanted to buy it to show my brother that you were not killed in the accident. I did not believe that you hated him because you were using the story of him in your artwork.

I wanted to show my bosses the quality of your sculptures, and it is very, very well done. Trinity Hotels would like to buy some land off of your father, including the spot and the Unspoken Garden. Trinity believes that the artwork in the garden path would be a draw for people to stay at the hotel. They would also like to implement a national skipping contest like they have in Franklin, Pennsylvania, and Red Bridge in the Allegheny National Forest, Pennsylvania.

Trinity figured it would help to fill the hotel a number of weeks in the year, making it a much more profitable hotel. The river walk, or Spot, as your family calls it, would be an excellent place for them to offer for weddings and receptions outside. It is a very beautiful setting, again, making the hotel much more profitable.

I will tell my employers at Trinity Hotels that the spot and the Unspoken Garden are way too precious for them to be able to purchase. They are having a little trouble raising all the money they need to build both hotels. I know they would still like to buy the land from you at a very good price. Will you please think about it?

BRUCE. We are not interested at all in selling any part of the Unspoken Garden or the spot.

(Niles read lips so if you face him, you two could talk.) It is time for me to go to the house.

SURELY, **signing.** If you will give me your word not to tell anybody about the back of the slates in the garden and give me your brother's name, I will make a slate for you.

NILES. No. I will not give you my word for a slate. I will not profit from hurting you or doing something that I should not have done in the first place. I give you my word, God as my witness. The knowledge of the back of the slates will not come from my mouth.

May God strike me deaf, and I never be able to hear you speak (smiles a little) if I tell about the back of the slates. My word is my bond, and God is my judge. Believe me when I tell you that, Surely.

SURELY, **signing**. Give me the name of your brother, and I will make a slate for him. Stop back in a few days. You know where to find me.

NILES. His name is Timothy.

58
Seven of Us

Surely arrived back up to the house an hour or so later. She told me that she had agreed to make a copy of the front of the slate with the boys and the bicycles for Timothy. Niles would be stopping back from time to time to see how far the work had progressed, then Niles would be taking the slate to Timothy. I was pleased that there was no ill will from Surely toward Timothy, knowing that he was one of the boys that caused the accident.

It seemed like every two or three days, Niles was there checking on the work being done on the slate. Niles talked to me each time about buying some of our land for the hotel. I told him that we are talking with the insurance companies, and it looked like we will be getting a good settlement from the accident. Therefore, we had no need what-soever to even consider selling the spot, the garden, Unspoken walkway, or part of the land.

I didn't know it took so long to make one of the slate pictures, but then of course, Surely and Pat were right in the middle of planting season. Pat was back working half days at the hotel, so it was taking longer to plant the garden.

We know by the scriptures there is a time set aside for all things, for planting and har-vesting, rejoicing and sorrows, work and rest. I guess the garden needed to be the priority at this time.

I know my work schedule goes later in the day than Niles's. It seems like every time he was there, he arrived an hour or so before I got home. Pat was good at putting him to work, helping in the garden or carrying slates for Surely, keeping him busy helping. He didn't seem to mind the work or helping.

I remember the one time coming home, Pat, Surely, and Niles were down back work-ing in the garden. Niles had taken off his dress shoes, socks, and his suit coat and put on knee pads (rubber pad that saves your knee when kneeling down on hard or rough surfaces) and he was pulling weeds in the garden, along with Surely and Pat.

I arrived home another time, and they were down back in the garden working. I was asked if I would go up and meet the pizza delivery. "Bring the pizza down with drinks so that we could all eat down at the spot." Niles had ordered and paid for a large double supreme from my favorite pizzeria. I will say he did know how to get to a man's heart. I don't know if he knew that was my favorite pizza and favorite pizzeria place.

As we were finishing eating:

NILES. I was asked by the three owners of Trinity Hotels if the three of you would meet with them Saturday after next, here at the spot, so they can see the garden and the artwork in the Unspoken walk- way. They would like to provide lunch so we can get to know each other person- ally. They would like to know and understand the importance of the spot and the Unspoken walkway to your family.

BRUCE. The spot has always been open for people to visit. We have had numerous friends here throughout the years. We are always interested in making new friends. We would be glad to meet with them, provided they know up front we have no interest whatsoever in selling the spot, the garden area, or the Unspoken walkway. Understand?

NILES. Yes.

That Saturday the seven of us met for lunch, talked, fellowshipped, and got to know each other personally. Time had gone by so fast. We called in an order for two large double supreme pizzas, two dozen chicken wings, and drinks from our favorite pizzeria for supper. At seven o'clock that evening, with a handshake, we had agreed to sell land, the Unspoken walkway, garden, and the spot to a franchise of the Trinity Hotel as soon as the attorneys could write up the paperwork.

59

Fullness of Time

Fourteen months after shaking hands on our agreements to sell some land, the Unspoken walkway, the garden, and the spot to the Trinity Hotel franchise, it became known as Trinity Hotels Love Garden

There was a grand opening. Each of the next five weekends, there were weddings planned in the hotel or in the garden, and there was a total of twelve weddings planned in the next six months. I have been putting in overtime for the last five months, getting the Love Garden property ready for occupancy and for the weddings and receptions that were going to be here, plus hiring six maintenance individuals to work in the three hotels and one assistant to help with purchasing of merchandise for all Trinity Hotels.

The last fourteen months had been an exciting time, and it looked as if Trinity Hotels research was right in their estimates of the amount of business that could be brought in to the area.

Pat was promoted and put in charge of the new banquet center that was in the Love Garden property space for four hundred people for a sit-down meal, plus catering for off-premises and catering for a hundred fifty people if they rented the garden spot. Pat managed a workforce of about eighteen people.

Pat hired one of her girlfriends from high school that had become widely known in the area for her cake decorating, wedding cakes, and cupcakes she made for individuals and events. Her name is Chelsea. You may not remember the name, but she was the girl back in school that asked Pat why she was whistling. They are still good friends.

Leroy was hired as assistant manager for the green house that was built on the side of the property. The greenhouse is to help supply flowers for the outside complex grounds and the garden spot, flowers for weddings, special events, and for the gift shop that is part of all the Trinity Hotel complexes. Also some vegetables that could be used in the kitchen were raised. It is a good drawing card for people that want fresh flowers and chemically free vegetables to eat at events.

Tony went to New York to study art but still has been offered to display for sale any of his original artworks in the gift shop. Josh has his local minister's license and is studying to be an ordained minister in the Evangelistic Calvary Baptist Church. Josh did his first wedding, plus his first wedding using sign in the ceremony.

Niles is the assistant manager for the Trinity Hotel Love Garden Complex and will probably become general manager of all the sites once Mr. Kiser retires. Not because he's marrying one of the majority shareholders in the Trinity Hotels Love Garden franchise, but because he is well qualified for the job. The proof is how he put this deal together to benefit everyone.

The first Saturday the hotel was in operation, Niles was getting what he wanted—his wedding to take place in the Love Garden Spot. It was only the second time a wedding had been performed at the spot. It was not to taking second place to his bride but the fact that his youngest brother was going to be his best man made the date, time, and place extremely special for the couple.

As I started to walk the bride down the path to where her mother and I got married and her soon-to-be husband stood waiting, Surely stopped, turned me so that we were face-to-face, and in a very soft but audible voice said,

SURELY. Surely know I love you, Dad, Mom, and Niles with all of my heart. God has surely blessed us.

I walked the bride down to her soon-to-be husband with tears in my eyes and gave her to him. I quietly took my seat by Pat. Josh came to the park for a ceremony where Surely was to respond by signing "I do." Instead, in a very soft audible voice:

SURELY. I do. Surely I love you, Niles.

You could hear a gasp from people that were in the front rows.

PAT. Praise the Lord.

Pastor Josh took off his glasses, wiping tears from his eyes before he could continue on with the ceremony. You should know that Josh and Surely have a very special bond of love.

Niles did not hear her, but he knew what she said by reading her lips. He knew it was audible by the response of the other people in the wedding party and responded by saying,

NILES. Surely know that I love you, Surely.

I could hear whispering going on behind me. Most people did not hear Surely's soft whisper but did hear Pat say, "Praise the Lord." They were just telling one another what had taken place.

60

Harvest

In the fullness of time, the union between the male and female, whether plant or animal or human, bring forth the harvest of that union combining the good and the bad of both the female and male.

Surely proved to be a hybrid having the best qualities of both—of course most of the best qualities came from her father.

All right, give me a break. I can't be incorrect all the time. There has to be at least one good quality that came from me. I do agree that most of the best qualities Surely exhibit came from Pat. It is yet to be determined all the qualities her brother has taken from each of us. He does have his sister to emulate or compete with and has shown some of the good qualities of both of his grandparents.

Bible states that in the fullness of time, a harvest will produce thirty-, sixty-, one-hundred-fold return of whatever has been planted. Harvest is not limited to just one season.

My dad would say anybody can count the number of seeds in an apple, only God knows how many apples are in a seed.

In some respects, Surely proved this also by making us grandparents some elven months after their wedding. She apparently didn't want to make a mistake by making Niles unhappy about not having a son or a daughter so she had twins. Not just twins, one of each a boy and a girl. How does that happen?

With strong encouragement to do so from her mother and good planning, they had picked out both a girl's and a boy's name.

61

Your Invitation to Become Part of the Family

Good planning can help you to become part of the most important family in the universe. The Royal family of I AM the GOD that created the universe invites you to be His son or daughter.

The most important part of this biography is that you might come to be able to see your heavenly Father working in your life. The Bible John 1, verse 12: "But as many as received him to them gave he the power to become the sons of God."

You can receive Jesus Christ as your Lord and Savior right now if you pray, expressing desire in your heart to have your sins forgiven and become part of the heavenly family.

Simple pray:

Lord Jesus, I believe I am lost and separated from you by my sins, and You are the only way to eternal life. I receive you as my Savior and Lord of my life and thank you for dying for me and paying the penalty of my sins that should be my death so that I can be part of the family of God.

You have planted the seed of God's love in your soul help it to grow and, in the fullness of time, to produce a harvest.

Read the Bible and affiliate yourself with a Bible-believing church.

God bless you and may you see GOD working in your life day by day. I pray we may get to meet each other sometime in eternity. God's blessing to you, brothers and sisters in Christ.

62
Sparks

These are a few sparks, or questions, if you prefer, hopefully looking at life in a little different way than usual and helping to start some discussion. This is not a test; you will not be graded on your answers. My prayer is that you will seek to understand the question before you give what you think is a correct answer. There can be many correct answers. The important part is why you gave what you think is a correct answer.

There is no particular order to the way the questions are being posed. Good luck. Have some fun.

1. Do you own a Bible?
2. Have you ever read the Bible?

3. The United States is based on the teachings that are in the Bible. Do you believe that those teachings have benefited the United States and its people?

4. Should people be held responsible for their actions?

5. Should parents deliberately let their children disobey them?

6. What is guidance?

7. What is abuse?

8. What is correction?

9. What is punishment?

10. Have you ever been attacked by an animal? How did it make you feel? What did you learn?

11. What are goals?

12. What makes up a goal?

13. Do goals benefit us, or how do they benefit us?

14. Have you ever skipped stones?

15. Do you judge people by their appearance, or should you?

16. What does it mean to be up a creek without a paddle?

17. Are good manners helpful in a society? Why or why not?

18. Answering a question, is honesty always the best policy?

19. Do you need to answer all questions that are asked of you?

20. Do we value people because of their gender?

21. Are there roles or duties that only one gender can do?

22. Do emotions affect us physically?

23. Is life too important to take seriously?

24. We all need help with something at some time in our life. True?

25. Why are females so hard to understand by men?

26. What are cooties and do boys really have them?

27. Should children be given or earn an allowance?

28. Why is lecturing not informing someone?

29. Why is it that when somebody says we need to talk, we usually think it is bad?

30. At what age do we become mature?

31. Are there consequences to all of our actions?
32. Are you romantic and what makes a person romantic?
33. What is the best way to help somebody when they are upset?
34. How open should we be to our mate about our feelings and emotions?
35. Have you ever asked God to guide and direct you? Why or why not?
36. Are you a dog-loving or a cat-loving person?
37. Have you ever been in an accident or a loved one been in an accident? Did you ask why?
38. What is your favorite holiday? Why and how do you celebrate it?
39. What are your special skills or abilities?
40. Would you rather get bad news from a friend or a stranger? Why?
41. How important is family to you?
42. Are you impatient about things in your life, or do you take them one day at a time?

43. Is patience a good thing? Why or why not?

44. Do you see God working in your life? Would you like to see him working in your life?

45. What is your favorite dessert or flavor of ice cream?

46. Does haste make waste?

47. Why do people name inanimate objects? Do you name objects?

48. If something tragic was to happen, would you rather it be to you or to your loved one? Why?

49. Which is most important to you: your sight, your hearing, or your speaking? why?

50. Do you know how to grow plants, and what is your favorite vegetable?

51. If someone tells you a secret and asked you to keep it, do you keep it? Why or why not?

52. Do actions speak louder than words?

53. Do we judge people by their actions or their words? Which is more import- ant? why?

54. How do you let people know you love them?

55. Is everything you have for sale? At what price would you sell?

56. What do you have or use to help you through the hard times in life?

57. Do you try to benefit from all the things you've done in your life?

58. Which is most important to you: fame, money, power, or relationships and why?

59. Will you make it a point in your life to let those people you love know how you feel?

60. What other questions do you think should have been asked?

61. Were there other questions brought to mind because of this book?

About the Author

The author works for his heavenly Father. He and his wife owned a fireworks business for some twenty-five years, selling fireworks wholesale and designing and producing firework shows. He was in sales and has written a number of sales training manuals prior to getting into the fireworks as a business.

He developed and produced a training class to help individuals be able to obtain permits to become legal in displaying fireworks in some states. He also wrote numerous legal briefs in his careers.

CPSIA information can be obtained
at www.ICGtesting.com
Printed in the USA
LVHW040705241120
672559LV00004B/180